GREEN SPACES

GREEN SPACES

Elizabeth Daish

This first world edition published in Great Britain 2001 by
SEVERN HOUSE PUBLISHERS LTD of
9–15 High Street, Sutton, Surrey SM1 1DF.
This first world edition published in the USA 2001 by
SEVERN HOUSE PUBLISHERS INC., of
595 Madison Avenue, New York, NY 10022.

British Library Cataloguing in Publication Data

Daish, Elizabeth
    Green spaces
    1. Love stories
    I. Title
    823.9'14 [F]

ISBN 0–7278–5678–2

Typeset by Palimpsest Book Production Limited,
Polmont, Stirlingshire, Scotland.
Printed and bound in Great Britain by
MPG Books Ltd, Bodmin, Cornwall.

One

"Oh, not again!" Penny turned away but it was too late. The three German tourists had seen her and waved as if they were her dearest friends. She made a dismissive gesture and tapped the dial of her wristwatch as if she had an appointment, but the determined-looking woman left the queue for entry tickets to the Museum of Costume and joined her, followed more slowly by her husband and the younger man.

"You will allow us to take a ticket for you?" she said.

"And after perhaps, you will join us for some coffee?" the tall young man said eagerly.

"You were so kind," the woman said slowly as if having to choose her words carefully. The other man, who Penny assumed was the father, said nothing but beamed and nodded, as if he was programmed to leave everything to his wife although he understood everything that was being said.

Penny managed to smile. "I only sorted out your money to buy stamps," she protested, and wanted to add: if you'd held up the queue much longer there would have been a riot!

"We have now understood the pound and the twenty pence piece," the woman said proudly. "Also the tiny coin that is worth little."

"Five p," Penny suggested.

"Why do you not have simple currency? But one day

1

you'll have the same as the rest of Europe," the young man said in an amused voice, as if it was incomprehensible that the British should want to hold out against the discussed single currency for a United Europe.

"How much these tickets are, please?" It was clear that Frau Braun would not let her go in a hurry and had a handful of money ready for Penny to inspect and sort out again. Inwardly, she sighed, but showed them which coins to use and discouraged them from offering a twenty pound note, as the girl behind the grille was having trouble with change and made irritated noises.

"For you, too?" Helmut Braun said hopefully and Penny recognised an interest that was not wholly for the culture that the city of Bath had to offer. He was good-looking, with firm smooth skin and good teeth and very humorous eyes, and she sympathised if he was tied to his dull parents for this holiday, but no way could she get sucked into their itinerary with all three of them and be bored out of her mind.

This is the first holiday I've had on my own for two years, she reminded herself when she felt a twinge of guilt at being selfish. This time I am doing what I want to do, and I don't have to look over my shoulder to see if I'm "fitting in" with the others. No more lame ducks, and no more sulks if I suggested an outing that Vincent wouldn't want to do.

Helmut smiled with sudden sweetness and she hesitated, but as he drew nearer to take the suggested change from his mother's hand Penny caught a whiff of the same aftershave that Vincent used and she hardened her heart.

"That is for three tickets," she said firmly. "I came to pick up a leaflet and to know the times of opening but I can't stay to go in now," she lied. "I have an appointment and can not spare the time now to see this museum, but thank you for offering to buy my ticket."

2

She found that she was speaking with exaggerated slowness to make them understand and, even so, only Helmut seemed to get the drift of what she was saying.

"This afternoon we visit the Roman Baths and have English tea in the Pump Rooms," Helmut said, referring to a leaflet and looking like a pleading spaniel at Penny, who shook her head and said firmly that she had her day planned.

Frau Braun smiled approval as she took in the simply cut skirt and Liberty silk shirt and good shoes, the smooth brown hair and the delicate complexion, and Penny had a terrifying vision of herself as being considered a suitable girl for Frau Braun's son to bring home.

"Must go," Penny said lightly. "See you around."

"Yes?" Helmut brightened. "Bath is not big. As you say, we shall meet again soon."

She stepped back from the queue and stood on the toe of the Japanese man who was standing uncomfortably close behind her. He apologised as if he was to blame and she almost apologised too when he bowed, but she just smiled faintly and backed away. It was his fault, she decided. He had been too close for comfort and good manners, standing almost on her heels. She moved away quickly and walked down the steep path from the museum. Not my morning for international *entente*, she thought.

It was disappointing. She had planned at least two hours this morning looking at costume through the ages, partly for pleasure and partly to see if anything caught her attention that could be used in her next dress collection, but it would have to wait until the next day when the German family had gone on to other venues. She laughed softly. At least I know that I shall not visit the Roman Baths today while they are there.

In a city as busy as Bath it had seemed odd at first to

see the same faces over and over again in the different tourist spots. But perhaps not, as they all wanted to see the same ancient treasures and fine buildings, and there were many groups organised by travel firms that covered most of the historic places and buildings of interest, in rigid itineraries.

I have leisure, she reflected, and felt good. I don't have to be shepherded in with a group. I have time alone for what I want to do, and if I don't want to do anything, then I can idle and waste time. A whole day in the Costume Museum tomorrow was something she'd enjoy and the Baths the day after would be fine, but she decided that today was far too sunny to waste it in dark rooms.

The sky, free of cloud, was a bright blue behind the heavy pink blossoms on the ornamental cherry trees. When she was four, Penny had stood under such a tree with her face upturned to catch the cool petals as they fell in the spring breeze. She had forgotten it until now but the warm sunshine and the soft fall of petals reminded her with sudden clarity. It could have been in the garden of her parents' home in Devon, her grandfather's house in Bristol, or the smaller garden of her Aunt Cathy in Hereford, but she remembered only the blossom and the feeling of rapture as she gazed up through the pink-tipped branches at the blue sky.

She paused under the tree, amused at recalling such trivial details as the fact that she wore a knitted red woollen hat and a thick anorak, which meant that the air was cool. It must have been Hereford she decided. Devon would have been warmer. What did it matter now? The child of that time had long outgrown knitted hats.

The remembered rapture vanished in a whiff of diesel fumes and she shrugged away the sudden unfamiliar nostalgia. Must be getting sentimental, she thought wryly, and rammed the wide-brimmed straw hat firmly on to her thick hair, but not so far gone as to stay with a bare head and have a red face and peeling nose under the now hot sun.

She crossed the busy street and walked down to the main shopping area. The shop fronts in Milsom Street were dusty and the smell of car fumes unpleasant and intrusive, although she was used to noisy smelly cities. Somehow here, it was sad. Bath was so beautiful and had known better times . . . and worse.

She imagined the shouts and the tramp of a Roman legion. No shops then with modern fashionable clothes, and no elegant cafés with good coffee and wickedly indulgent Mikados, the conical sponge cakes spilling cream and dark chocolate, or Bath Olivers, Bath buns and Sally Lunn cakes, that had helped to make Bath a special tourist centre from Regency times onwards.

She stopped by a shop window framed in carved mahogany and showing unusual furniture, handcrafted by local artists. The drapes at the back of the display were boldly designed and pleasing, and Penny wondered who had made them and if she could buy them . . . for what?

Her shoulders slumped wearily and the emotions that she thought were firmly under control threatened to surface. There was no longer a place for such things. The old house that she had shared with Vincent and his friends Margie and William was a figment of the past, unreal as it had been on the day they all moved out, leaving bare rooms after the ruthless sale of every stick of furniture and every rug and curtain that had been bought in sale rooms and for which they'd shared the cost in the first enthusiasm for furnishing the house together. As Margie insisted, they must sell everything and the money could be evenly divided.

At the time, Penny was glad to let it all go, but since then she wished she had bid for a few items that she had enjoyed using when she lived with Vincent.

Stupid! she told herself. Where would it fit in at the studio where she worked and was now camping out until she found a small apartment?

She looked at silver in another window, aware of its beauty but glad she'd resisted the offer of a cabinet of ornate and mainly unusable pieces that an aunt had offered her, who had been hurt when she'd announced, "Thank you but no, life is too short to polish silver." Vincent had been furious and mentally totted up what they might have been worth at auction but, as Penny pointed out, if she had accepted them she couldn't sell them as Aunt Monica would expect to see them whenever she popped in on her rare visits to London.

Vincent was mean, she recollected, mostly in little things. And he was very selfish, but they had been fairly contented, and she couldn't remember when it had all begun to fall apart, her life with Vincent and her good relationship with the other couple. She passed a grille in a café wall through which an aromatic wave of freshly ground coffee filled the air, inviting the tourists to go into the café and indulge themselves with coffee and fattening cakes.

After the break-up there had been too many mornings sipping coffee and staring at the middle distance and now she avoided such places if she was alone, using cafés only when she was really hungry.

It had been late December with Christmas just round the corner when they left the house. She smiled wryly. Islington had never been her ideal home base but work and Vincent had tied her there for two years and the house had been big enough to divide conveniently so that the two couples could have a degree of privacy and yet live together in the main rooms in harmony.

Apart from the obligatory hand on her knee but never higher, when William drank more than his ration of whisky, and Vincent's one-night stand with Margie when they first moved in – an episode never repeated as Margie, who lacked variety in her marriage, had wanted more than Vincent could offer – life had settled down to tranquillity, almost to the edge of boredom.

Looking back, Penny found it difficult to believe that she'd accepted a lover who did little for her own libido and tried to dominate her gently in an almost fatherly way.

"Isn't he sweet," her friends would say and it was true at first, when Penny revelled in a calm and neutral setting with a man in the background who kept the wolves at bay, but Margie grew restless and wanted to live in Tuscany for a year to paint farmhouses and to sample the local male talent, or, as she put it, she wanted warmth. William, as usual, shrugged away anything he wanted to do, packed his laptop and followed.

Suddenly the whole set-up fell apart. Margie wanted to leave as soon as possible and Vincent had been offered a part in an American soap that might just make him famous.

"We can leave in the New Year," he announced calmly one evening, as if suggesting a visit to the opera or a Chinese restaurant – something pleasant to do but hardly mind-bending.

"We?" Penny asked through gritted teeth.

He looked surprised. "You can do your little designs as easily there as here," he said indulgently. "The Americans will love them."

"Did it occur to you that I might not want to live in America?" she asked with false sweetness. "As for my *little* designs; if you recall, they paid the bills for quite a time while you were resting last year."

Vincent went red and looked away. "We are an item now," he said. "We are a team, darling. Where I go, you go too." He saw that she was not impressed. "Once we are there, I can take the strain and pay for everything if that's what you want. We could even get married," he added generously.

"What a delightful proposal. I don't care about money. You should know that. I just like to be consulted and it would be a change if you didn't take me for granted. Would you do the same for me if we were moving out and away for my work? What if I said I wanted to live in Paris for a year? It's on the cards that I could take a studio right in the middle of the fashion scene and be right there for the collections and loads of contacts." She hated her own voice as it grew shrill.

"That's impossible. I've accepted and we leave mid January," he snapped. "Besides, I hate Paris."

"You've bloody signed and never mind my life being disrupted?"

"I thought you'd be pleased," he said plaintively. "It's the peak of my career so far and it will lead to wonderful things . . . for both of us," he added.

"Not for both of us, Vincent. I always knew you were a selfish bastard but it didn't really affect me as I was free to do what I wanted, but now I doubt if I even like you very much. I am not coming with you and Margie is right. We must sell up everything and go our separate ways."

"You'll calm down and know that what I have planned is right for us," he said, but she saw that he was shaken.

"I'll see Margie. We seem to be the only ones who have any business sense round here. Why don't you go and play over the videos they sent you of the soap? For the umpteenth time," she said acidly. "You can act as prompt for the others in the cast when you get to the States."

He thought she added "Narcissus," but he kept quiet, very disturbed by her attitude and not all that hopeful that he could talk her round.

In bed that night she'd pretended to be asleep when he

8

tried to put his arms round her, and yet she longed to be held! – but not by Vincent. I've wasted time, she thought. How easy it would be to go to America, enjoy a little luxury and vegetate, but her outburst had released something that had smouldered for ages and she knew that she was on her own.

"On my own," she murmured in the hot sunshine, but now she said it with satisfaction. She had accepted Vincent as a prop and a less than satisfactory bed companion, but after the row they'd discovered that their life together was unimportant to both of them, amiable and affectionate though it had been. Habit would have made us stay together and we might have got married and been a fairly average couple, a marriage of convenience with a so-called normal existence.

Penny took a deep breath. I've escaped but I have no idea what to do, she thought. It's true that I can design anywhere and I'd like to travel but not to Cannes and the places where Vincent might meet film directors and producers. She almost envied Maggie, who had hinted that she wanted a bit on the side, a bit of rough to give a little excitement to her life. But it wasn't sex she wanted, just change and beauty. She pictured Vincent's good-looking, round face and the flamboyant bow ties he wore, and felt no regrets at leaving him even if he had been a haven to which she could go if other men became pushy.

I'm lazy and I don't want even a mild flirtation just now, she decided. The German was obviously interested and there had been a lot of glances at her good legs and lithe body as she walked down towards the Abbey.

She skirted the Abbey precincts, unwilling to be seduced by its splendour until the skies were grey and Bath assumed a veil that hid its beauty. The sunken garden by the river was a mass of blossom, and deck-chairs and loungers were scattered over the grass. The view of the weir under Pulteney Bridge was one of her favourite sights and she paid for her entrance to the gardens and walked down the path and under the trees. A stall selling soft drinks and wrapped sandwiches seemed a good idea and she bought her lunch to eat in solitude, slinging her squashy handbag under the wooden recliner chair and settling with her face to the sun.

No culture vultures, no foreign voices, no pushy students and no noise or fumes. The filigree of light through the blossom would make a good design for next spring's fabrics if made in more muted colours. She sighed with pleasure. She had finished and found markets for her autumn collection and had a breathing space and money, but she made a note for her fabric designer and a quick sketch before opening her sandwich pack.

Music from a lunch-hour band made her look up. Uniformed musicians under the ornate Victorian bandstand played carefully chosen tunes from old musicals and light classics, adding to the ambience of the old city and making no concessions to the brash music of the very young.

Bath had been a good choice for her break. There was so much to do and yet plenty of places where a female alone could relax without being hassled. She pulled the ring on the can of fizzy orange and held the can at arm's length to avoid being splashed by the gush of sweet sticky fluid released with the pressure.

A few more people came to sit on the deck-chairs and listen to the music, and a man stretched his lean length on the grass close to where she sat, but he seemed oblivious to his surroundings and certainly paid no attention to the woman eating chicken sandwiches, her face almost hidden under the straw hat.

Music and the soft sunladen air made her sleepy so she extended the footrest and tilted the chair back to a relaxing angle. Her head fell to one side and, through half-closed eyes, she saw the man under the tree. He was half-asleep too, and petals were falling on his head. He was as relaxed as a puppy, with every muscle loose and natural in sleep. Penny stifled a laugh as one whole floret fell into his open mouth. He coughed and sat up, looking cross and disbelieving that such a thing could happen to him.

He saw her laughing and gave a reluctant grin. "Any left?" he asked, pointing to the can on the grass. He coughed again. "Some went down the wrong way." Penny held out the nearly full can that she had found too sweet to quench her thirst and he tipped it up and drank until the can was empty.

"Yuck," he said. "How can you drink that stuff?"

"You just did," she reminded him. "I left it because I didn't like it." She couldn't place his accent but thought it might be Canadian or possibly Australian.

As if sharing a can of fizz made them acquainted, he came closer. "I'm Jake," he said. His grey eyes were full of humour. "No, I'm not an Aussie or a Canadian as all you Limeys think. I'm a Kiwi. New Zealand," he explained kindly.

"I have heard of the place," Penny conceded solemnly, and added reluctantly, "I'm Penny."

"And you are British?"

"I am British and this is the city of Bath, in England," she answered mildly. "We haven't been taken over completely by tourists."

"You could have fooled me. Each time I ask the way I'm met with blank stares or at best the one phrase they all know: 'Sorry, I am not English.'"

Penny laughed. "I know the feeling from the other side, but fortunately the orientals are easy to spot. The continental Europeans are not so easy. I've just been sorting out money for a family of Germans."

"And you escaped to the peace and quiet of these gardens?"

"That's right." She leaned back and pushed her hat over her face. "I came here to be completely alone. Goodbye, Jake."

"Ouch!" he said. He levered himself up and took the empty can to the rubbish bin, and when she peeped out from under the hat brim he had gone.

Two

It was very quiet. Penny pushed aside her hat, and the view up through the branches wasn't inviting. The sky had drained its blue as if a water colourist was tired of its intensity and preferred a wash of grey. The few remaining blossoms on the tree looked sad and the wide band of pink petals on the grass round the bole of the tree was the only vibrant colour left.

The bandsmen were packing up their brass instruments and drums and most of the visitors had left the gardens. Penny dragged a light sweater from her bag and struggled into it. A glance at her watch told her that she had been asleep for over two hours; she was thirsty. The cloying sweetness of the canned drink had left her dry but the kiosk was closing as the first drops of rain fell and it was obvious that there would be no more customers wanting refreshments until the sun shone again.

Hurriedly she packed her bag with her notebook and the paperback she had not yet opened and scanned the grass to make sure she had left nothing behind. She almost ran for the exit. The small cafés on the bridge were nearest and she hoped there would be a vacant seat in one of them.

"Not the real thing," the woman on the other side of the small table said, cutting open a fruity concoction that masqueraded as a Bath bun. Penny examined the tea menu and the woman turned to the Swedish couple on the adjoining table. "I should know. I live here, but can I get into the real Bath Bun Café? Not until all the foreigners have left."

"This is good." The man looked puzzled. "We came here yesterday and like this food." The woman realised that the blond, well-dressed couple were not British and sniffed. "If you had the real thing you'd know the difference, but I suppose you know no better."

Penny felt almost responsible for the rude tone and smiled at the couple. "They do make wonderful Maids of Honour tarts here," she told them. "Each café has something good and maybe something not so good." She ordered two Maids of Honour and Darjeeling tea, and found that once again she was considered to be the fount of all knowledge as far as Bath was concerned.

The woman at her table left, with a scathing look at the Swedish couple, who promptly moved over to take her place and the other vacant chair. "It is permitted?" asked the blonde woman.

Why don't I keep my big mouth shut? Penny wondered, but she smiled and said, "Feel free."

They looked puzzled. Back to words of one syllable, no vernacular and speaking at a snail's pace, Penny decided. At least Jake had been easy. A twinge of regret made her wish she'd been nicer to him. It was ironic that the fact that he'd sensitively accepted her need to be alone made him more attractive than if he'd pushed his luck. He didn't have smelly trainers and his shirt was clean.

The Swedes were going through a handful of brochures and showed every sign of making the most of their captive Brit. Penny advised suitable tours in the Mendip Hills and Cheddar Gorge, where they would have no need to speak at all, and the American Museum on the hill overlooking Bath if the weather was bad, but thought that the play in the local theatre might be beyond their comprehension unless they had mastered the art of four-letter words as punctuation in each sentence.

As they relaxed, Penny saw that they were pathetically grateful for her help but once again she wanted to push strangers away with stiff outstretched arms as they invaded her space. She had no place to hide, no Vincent with whom she could invent a date and, if she was honest, no real plans that gave her much pleasure, no outing with an interesting companion to which she looked forward with eagerness.

"We go to London next week," Gertrude said, and Penny found herself describing what she thought they might enjoy there. "You know London very well." It was a statement, not a question, as Penny became enthusiastic about monuments and exhibitions that had never really impressed her a lot when she lived in Islington but now seemed warm and familiar and friendly. She had to admit that she'd never seen the exhibits in the Royal Collection in Buckingham Palace or been down to Kew in lilac time, a lapse that gave her a black mark, but she suggested several musicals that might interest them.

"You are alone?" She nodded. "That is bad at night." She raised her eyebrows and Lars laughed. "Not for bed, but earlier."

"During the evenings?"

"That is so. You will dine with us tonight? Our hotel is good and close to the Abbey."

Penny opened her mouth to refuse politely, then saw Jake in the doorway eyeing the full tables and frowning until a waitress showed him an empty place. He grinned and sat down a few yards away from Penny.

"How kind," Penny said. "I'd like to have dinner in your company but you must let me buy the wine."

"We are very pleased," Lars said. "Sometimes we find it a strain trying to be understood but with you, we are good."

He looked at the cuckoo clock on the wall. "We meet at seven? Now we go inside the Abbey." He picked up his bill and they wandered off to the desk to pay, leaving two seats vacant again.

Penny wished she'd not ordered two Maids of Honour tarts as one had remained uneaten while she talked to the Swedes, and she saw that Jake had noticed her. If I leave now it looks as if I'm in a panic, she thought, and felt annoyed. Why should she feel anything of the sort? He was just a man who almost swallowed a bunch of blossoms and he was not important.

"Hi there," Jake said cautiously, recalling the peremptory way he had been dismissed in the gardens. He put a hand on the back of one frail cane chair and looked at Penny hopefully.

The diffident small boy expression might be a stock in trade but Penny decided that it worked, and laughed. "Sit down if you must," she said. "Don't loom over me; and shouldn't it be Kia Ora, not hi there?"

"You've been down under?" he asked eagerly.

"No, I watch a lot of soaps." She recollected Vincent trying out a Kiwi accent before an audition and the number of times she had to hear his lines.

"What's that you're eating?"

"Order your own," Penny said sharply as he leaned over as if to sample her Maid of Honour tart.

"You shared your drink with me."

"You scavenged my leftovers. This is different." She cut the tart and showed him the light egg and fruit filling, and he pointed to her plate when the waitress came to take his order.

"Three like that, and coffee."

"Three Maids of Honour. Yes, sir," the girl said and fluttered her eyelashes at him.

16

"I've never devoured four virgins in one afternoon," he said wickedly, and glanced at Penny as if testing her reaction.

"Don't believe all that history tells you," she said calmly. "But a lot did go on in those boudoirs whether or not the Maid of Honour was willing. Substitute rape for coming to the aid of a maiden in distress and you'll be closer to the truth. Isn't it nice that today a girl can say no, and a man knows she means it?"

"Three Maids of Honour, and coffee," the waitress said and put the tray down on the table.

"I think he wants four," Penny said sweetly. "That's what the man said. He wants an extra tart."

"Three's plenty," Jake said hastily. "I don't want indigestion."

Penny regarded him with an amused lift to the corners of her mouth and decided that he was not a threat. His face was pink and he stuffed a whole tart into his mouth to hide his embarrassment.

He swallowed hard and drank some coffee. "Are you always so sharp?" he asked.

"You'll never know," she replied and gathered up her bag and the folding umbrella she carried in her holdall and made for the pay desk.

"Penny?" he called. "Have dinner with me tonight?"

"I already have a date," she said and paid her bill.

The rain had stopped and she walked back to her rented apartment, kicked off her damp shoes and put the kettle to boil. Then turned it off again. I'm awash with tea, she decided, and Vincent isn't likely to come in demanding coffee. The small sitting-room needed extra light when the sun went in and the ancient standard lamp had a silk shade that cast a jaundiced brightness over the yellow rose-patterned armchairs. Penny dragged a chair to the window so that she could watch the people passing on their way home from offices and the trail of red rear lights as the traffic flow slowed down by the junction.

I'm a towny, she decided. The park had been wonderful but all parks in cities were good. She needed to see people and traffic and old buildings. She began to read her new paperback, with the background of Bath in the rush hour humming gently and reassuringly through the window.

A church clock struck the half hour after six and she had to shower and change quickly, putting on a silk shift of deep turquoise and adding a simple rope of fake pearls with gold links. She knew the hotel where Lars and his wife were staying and it was one of the best in Bath. A long silk raincoat would cope with any shower on her way home and she made sure she had enough ready money and a plastic card for wine and a taxi if she needed one.

Penny arrived at the hotel with two minutes to spare and tidied her hair before she pushed on the revolving door to the foyer. To her surprise she felt lighthearted and pleased to have an evening out with a couple who would make no demands and might even be good company.

The couple were waiting by the desk and smiled as soon as they saw her. "We are so pleased," Gertrude said. "We thought you might not come. You must have many friends here with whom you eat dinner."

"Not many," Penny said. "I was asked by a New Zealander I met today but this is better."

Looking about her, Penny almost wished she had decided to stay in a hotel, as the decor here was far better than the rather dreary setting of the apartment, but she had needed a place where she would have her own front door key to lock out the world and be able to relax in a dressing-gown if she wanted to breakfast late. Also, she had a private telephone in a quiet place and once she had done the usual touristy things she might, just might, want to contact Josie and talk shop and discuss any ideas they had for the next dress collection.

In a large hotel, the temptation to use a fax machine might be too much and she could get entangled with other business people in the bar or coffee lounges. Very few people knew her address in Bath and with no electronic wizardry there was no chance of them faxing her, so in many ways the arrangement was ideal, but she had to admit that an evening with really dry Martinis or something smooth on the rocks, in good glass, and later, she hoped, a meal served with care and panache, would make a change from takeaways in the apartment, sandwiches in the park and cans of undrinkable fizz. She gave in to a feeling of complete self-indulgence.

Gertrude eyed her dress with approval and asked the name of the maker.

"It's one of mine," Penny said and it was too late to keep quiet about what she did for a living.

Lars glanced at his wife and grinned. "My wife loves clothes and has her own business designing accessories."

Gertrude said something sharply in their own language and Penny sensed that it was somewhat rude. "He promised me not to tell anyone what I do," she said in English. She laughed. "We may be, as you say, in the same yacht? I think you live in an apartment to avoid people like me!"

"Not people like you," Penny replied. "Just the ones who have never made anything in their lives but who try to tell me that a shift like this is overpriced and so simple that they could run one up on a machine in one evening if they had the time."

Lars groaned. "I need a drink," he said. "What would you like, Penny?"

The two women looked amused and Penny said, "It was you who mentioned Gertrude's work and I let my tongue slip, too, but I promise not to talk shop for more than three hours! I'd like a vodka and tonic, please."

"I shall bring the drinks and expect to talk about Bath, not dresses and scarves and handbags, when I return. They are busy now, so I will go to the bar."

"Is he really upset if you talk about your work?"

Gertrude smiled. "Lars is the one who talks, but tonight he is amused that you were the guilty one. He is very proud of my success and would say more if I allowed. We have four boutiques and he gave up his accountancy work and now works for the firm."

"You are so lucky," Penny said.

"You are not married, I think?"

Penny saw that she eyed her ringless hands. "No, I lived with someone but we have finished and he is in America."

"You are unhappy?"

"No. I am enjoying my freedom."

"But you are in danger of taking someone to fill his place?"

"Danger? I think not," Penny said shortly.

"It is a bad time, between lovers," Gertrude said calmly. "You could take the wrong man because you miss something." She looked at the smooth oval face and the lively mouth and laughed softly. "You have no need to . . . what is it I want to say? When a woman has fear that she is ugly and will have no more men to be lovers?"

Penny shrugged and smiled slightly. "Panic is the word I suppose. As yet I have avoided men with that look in their eyes."

"The man in the café?"

"Who?" But Penny knew she meant Jake.

"I said to Lars that he wanted to eat you and not his Bath buns."

"I don't know him. I met him in the park and he drank

20

my orange drink." Gertrude looked puzzled so Penny told her what had happened.

"Run to us if he follows you and you do not want," Gertrude said. "We are here for a few more days and he will move on also." She looked thoughtful. "He is good-looking and has humour, I think. You need a companion who does not make you have a wanting for him. That is until you find a man you can trust and love."

"I may not want another lover," Penny said, and wished she understood Swedish when Gertrude looked scornful and dismissed her remark with one terse phrase.

Lars appeared with a laden tray and they talked of Bath and the surrounding countryside until it was time to go in for dinner.

Penny felt a welcome affinity with these strangers. I can meet some people every day for years and never want to know them more deeply and yet I feel an instant rapport with Gertrude, she decided, and after dinner when they sat in the deep velvet chairs in the lounge and drank coffee and liqueurs, they exchanged home addresses and showed a firm mutual business interest that pointed to Gertrude supplying some accessories for the next winter collection.

More people came into the lounge as the theatre crowds left for their hotels and homes. Penny watched them and wondered what the Japanese party had made of the very odd play now showing. It was hardly Shakespeare or *Dear Octopus* and not even something between the two. She knew that the theatre would have been filled with coach parties, as the organisers booked the theatre, whatever was showing, to fill one evening of a tour.

"I don't think they enjoyed their evening as much as I have," Penny said. "If many English people find that play impossible to understand, how can anyone not speaking the language hope to do so?"

Elizabeth Daish

"You saved us from that," Lars said. "We visit the theatre whenever we can and would have gone there tonight if you had not told us it was bad."

"Oh dear!" Penny said softly. The German family were sitting by a statue and Frau Braun looked as cross as the marble nymph who was holding on to a very inadequate moulded drape. Her husband ignored her displeasure and made for the bar while Helmut spoke in resigned but faintly exasperated tones to his mother.

"Do you know them?" asked Gertrude. "Do you want to greet them?"

"No! I met them in the post office and again in a queue for the Costume Museum and sorted out their money. They tried to adopt me," she added with a smile.

"Just like us. We would adopt you, too. How you must not like foreigners taking your time," Gertrude said, teasing her.

"No, not a bit like you," Penny said firmly. "This has been a wonderful evening and I feel that we might see each other again soon."

"That makes me happy," Gertrude said. "If you want to escape that family, tell them you are with us and that we insist you come with us everywhere." She laughed. "Being Teutonic they will believe it, as I think they live like that. The son appears good and very patient, but I think they watch him all the time."

"He did seem nice," Penny said. "I wonder how he'd be without his family breathing down his neck."

"They do that? Is it a custom like animals breathing each other?" asked Lars, and laughed.

"I think you know exactly what I mean," Penny said.

"It is a good phrase and I shall remember and use it when I speak English in Sweden," Lars said with satisfaction. He leaned forward and whispered. "I think he breathes down your neck now."

22

Penny was aware of a shadow across the small table and turned when Helmut came into view. "Excuse me," he said, and then seemed to be at a loss, realising that Penny was with the people at the same table, not just sitting in the lounge having coffee.

"Hallo." Her smile was faint and lacked warmth. "Gertrude, this is someone I met briefly this morning."

"You are not alone?" He sounded disappointed, then smiled. "But you are staying here at this hotel? We are here, also."

"No. I am just visiting friends while they are in Bath," Penny said. "I have an apartment for a few days."

"You didn't go to the Costume Museum? I went back later alone but you were not there."

"We may go later but it depends on what my friends want to do," Penny said firmly.

Gertrude smiled. "We do as you say, Penny. We see so little of you that it doesn't matter where you want to go so long as we come too."

"You are Penny? I am Helmut," he said determined not to let her go that easily.

"I know. I heard your mother call you by name this morning. I think she may call you again. She looks anxious," Penny added, and turned away from him to sip her Cognac.

He paused irresolutely, then went back to his table, said a few words to his mother and walked rapidly to the elevators.

"Poor man," Gertrude said. "I can see that you are able to send men away, but he is worth some attention." She chuckled. "However, you do well to avoid having his mother . . . breathing down your neck."

"I think I'll go now," Penny said. "It's later than I thought possible but it's been a lovely evening."

"If the rain has not come, we can walk with you to keep

away all strange men," Lars said. "I like to see the weir at night and there might be a moon."

Frau Braun eyed them sourly as they left the lounge. Somehow, they had put her usually docile son in a bad mood and he had been almost rude to her, saying he wanted time alone and would see her in the morning.

Three

The Abbey needed no floodlighting under the nearly full moon and the spray tossed up by the weir gleamed silver over the dark water. "This is a good place and I wish we could stay for a month," Gertrude said.

"We have our own good buildings and many rivers," Lars reminded her.

She laughed. "Lars is afraid I might want to live in England or Paris or even America."

"With easy transport, there is no need," Penny said. "I love travelling but my home is here in England, I think."

"You are not sure?"

"I suppose I have to make up my mind about a lot of things," Penny said slowly. "I have no house or apartment in London now apart from my studio, and although I was raised there, I haven't lived in Devon for years. University changed my life and my parents now live in Canada with my brother and his wife, so I am footloose and fancy-free and could live anywhere." She saw that Lars was listening carefully. "OK! Let me rephrase that! I am free to choose and have no real plans," she added.

"Will you live with Vincent again, this time in America?"

"No, that is finished," she said firmly.

"Already in Bath you have met two men of different nations and will meet others in your work," Gertrude said. "You may want to marry someone from a different culture."

"I'd need to take a long hard look at his mother first! I think that poor Helmut will have to find someone who Frau Braun accepts, someone from a similar background, or he'll have to run away."

"He has a firm chin and good kind eyes," Gertrude said.

"Just as well that I shall never see him again." Penny smiled and her tone was mocking. "What a good thing I shall not have you breathing down my neck to make a marriage for me. What about Jake? He has nice eyes too, and we do speak the same language."

"You speak the same words, yes, but that is all," Gertrude said calmly. "Inside he is not like you."

Lars gave a sigh. "It is time we took you home and Gertrude gave up seeing too much. She is a witch when the moon shines."

"Really, truly?"

"Sometimes I see things," Gertrude admitted and laughed softly. "Now I do see a man who is not a vision and who does not want to be seen."

Penny glanced towards a shadow by the box-like building on the bridge that once was used as a bridewell to house drunks and cut-purses in the bad old days when the local militia locked them up pending their delivery to the law courts in the morning. She looked away quickly and the shadow faded.

"He follows you," Lars said. "Do I speak to him? It is not polite to follow you."

"Leave it, Lars, but thank you for seeing me safely home."

They quickened their steps and when Penny put her key in the lock Lars stared back at the empty street. "Go in and lock your door," he told her. "We shall walk back that way again and look."

"Are you sure you saw someone?" Penny asked. "It was

26

dark just there and if there was a man it could have been anyone."

"I'm sure," Gertrude asserted. "I have the eyes of a cat and I saw Helmut Braun."

"Good-night," Penny said, and when she had bolted the door she stared at the heavy oak panels and shivered, annoyed that she felt scared.

She made coffee that she didn't need and sat in darkness looking out of the window. I'm neurotic, she told herself. I've been followed home many times by students who fancied me, and there was the time when a Middle Eastern language student pursued me for two months, unable to believe I'd resist his charms, but that was usually in daylight, when he flaunted his lovely car and dangled the possibility of luxury before my bemused eyes.

She managed a short laugh and felt better. Vincent would love this situation. He would preen his ego and say she wasn't safe to be left alone for five minutes, and he knew she should never have left him. Why not change her mind and come to America?

Groups of people passed below the window, safe in each other's company and making more noise than they would if they were not on holiday. She envied them and almost wished she'd taken up Barbara's heavy hints and invited her to join her in Bath, but even a day with her was wearing, with her incessant talk of plays and very avant fringe theatre.

Barbara was a friend of Vincent's, who designed theatre stage sets and had made it plain that she thought Penny was mad to let him go. Most of Penny's so-called friends, apart from the ones from home and university, had been friends of Vincent; the places they had visited had been of his choosing; and even newspapers had been chosen by him and brought home rather than Penny having her choice delivered to the house.

What kind of a wimp does that make me? she thought wryly. For a few minutes she had wanted Vincent to be there, sprawled across the faded ochre velvet settee, drinking her coffee because he couldn't be bothered to make his own.

She sipped the now cold coffee and put the mug down on the small papier mâché table. Whoever Gertrude had seen was not outside now and she realised that she was tired and her unease was quite out of character. She washed the coffee mug and left it on the kitchen table to be used for breakfast. She stifled a sharp cry when the phone rang and she let it ring five times before she picked up the receiver.

"Hallo," she said, giving no indication of her identity or the phone number. It was too late for friends in London to ring for a chat and very few people knew where she was staying in Bath. She had once given her phone number automatically, late at night, and had been pestered for weeks by the same man ringing her number, after he had first made that random nuisance call, just dialling a number not knowing who would reply.

"Penny? I hope you were not in bed?"

"Gertrude!" Her relief was acute and to her seemed ridiculous.

"We wondered if you were relaxed? We saw your friend and said good-evening and asked him to join us with a drink. He couldn't refuse," she said dryly. "So we took him back to the hotel and now I think he is asleep."

"Did he get as far as this house? Did he see where I live?"

"No, we met him at the end of the road and all the houses look the same in that row, so he couldn't be sure which one you went into."

"Thank you," Penny said and found that she had been holding her breath.

"Do not worry about him," Gertrude said. "We talked and he is lonely."

"Surely he is old enough to have a holiday alone or with friends?" Penny gathered courage now and could afford to be scathing. "How can he put up with that terrible woman?"

Gertrude chuckled. "The lady is not his mother. She is the wife of his father after his mother died. She nursed his real mother and took over the family."

"His stepmother."

"It explains," Gertrude said. "She likes to be asked what they may do and it is as if she thinks they owe her more than she owes them and considers them ungrateful."

"Helmut told you all this?"

"A little. He is I think ready to leave, but his father would have to deal with her alone and that makes him sad."

"A bad case of moral blackmail," Penny said.

"A good phrase. I must write it for Lars for his collection."

"You are going to Cheddar tomorrow? I'd like to give you both dinner if you are back before eight? I can book a table in that restaurant by the Abbey."

"We return at seven, so that would be good, and we can tell our news to each other."

"I shall spend time in the Costume Museum and not have to avoid anyone!"

"If you see Helmut, be kind. He is a good man and needs friends. His mother died last year after a long illness and he feels as a bird in a cage."

"Trapped? I know the feeling," Penny said. "See you at eight. Good-night and thank you, Gertrude."

She set her alarm for seven a.m. Each morning she enjoyed Bath and the elegant backstreets before the city became noisy and full of tourists, and for her this was the best of the day. The gentle greys and pale yellows of Bath stone against the blue sky and the backdrop of huge trees in the parks filled her with wonder at the craftsmanship and love that had sculpted the houses and the pinnacles of the Abbey.

Even the smaller churches had this mark of care, and in one, when she climbed to the tower to see across the city, she had noticed an ornate flagstone in the wall of the loft, lovingly picking out the date and the name and trade of the mason who had helped to build the tower. The gargoyles were crafted as if they would be seen every day at ground level and the wooden racks that held the church bells would have been elegant in a drawing-room. How many people did see them in a whole lifetime? Just the birds, and the workmen who checked the bells on the upper platform, and a few inquisitive people like her who had the time and energy to climb the winding stone stairs.

She awoke to bird song and a fine day and dressed simply in a silk overshirt of dusky pink, designer jeans and soft blue leather moccasins. She bent the straw hat into some semblance of shape after its night rolled up in her holdall and grabbed her purse and sunglasses, determined to walk to the Crescent and back before eating breakfast in a café overlooking the weir.

Even the line of parked cars could not detract from the beauty of the Regency Crescent. The wide curve of town houses swept behind manicured lawns and ancient trees, and it was easy to imagine that gleaming carriages had drawn up to the houses, spilling out the high society of Bath, dressed in the silks and velvets and brilliant plumage of the era of the Prince Regent.

As always, Penny thought of the clothes, and reluctantly she dragged herself away to eat breakfast before going on to the Costume Museum.

The smell of fresh croissants and coffee lured her to the

café where she had met Gertrude and Lars and she found a table by the window. Butter in a pretty ceramic pot with a silver butter knife, a jar of honey and one of home-made marmalade bore no resemblance to the impossible-to-open plastic cases of rationed butter and preserves that now were almost universal in restaurants. Even the sugar was in three pots, one of white sugar, one of demerara and one of hard coffee sugar crystals. With the guilt of a child about to be caught in the act, Penny popped a brown crystal into her mouth and sucked it. It tasted as she remembered and her pleasure was complete.

"May I?"

Penny looked up sharply. The café was half empty and there was plenty of room for individuals to have separate tables. She looked pointedly at the empty tables and then relented. "If you must," she said, and looked out of the window.

"What are you having?"

"Breakfast," she said shortly. "Breakfast alone with my thoughts, so do you mind?"

"Pardon me for living," Jake said. "I hate sulky women."

The waitress came to take their orders. "Croissants and coffee please and I'll have my bill now as I'm in a hurry." The girl looked at Jake. "We are not together," Penny said firmly and pulled out a brochure for the caves in the Gorge at Cheddar that she'd meant to give to Gertrude but had forgotten.

"I'll have the same and some toast and Vegemite."

"Sorry, sir, I can get you Marmite, but not what you asked for," the girl said.

Jake gave her a devastating smile. "Call yourself a civilised country and you don't go for my favourite spread? I'll stick with croissants."

Penny continued reading about the souvenir shops that

31

she hoped she'd never have to visit, and ignored him. The girl eyed her with disbelief. If he was trying a pick-up, then she must be mad to brush him off. He had a gorgeous voice and a smile like that guy in "Neighbours". Give me the chance! she thought, and made sure that he had the best of the croissants and a really full pot of coffee.

Jake sat watching Penny's face, an enigmatic smile making his mouth curl up at the corners. It was a very attractive smile, Penny conceded, and she put the brochure away.

"Well, that's enough about me," Jake said, breaking a silence that had lengthened to ten minutes. "Tell me, Penny, what do you like doing, if you like anything at all?"

In spite of her intended resistance, she smiled. "I don't know you Jake and I don't think I want to know you. I came to Bath to have a quiet rest and recharge my batteries."

"With your face and figure, that is impossible," he replied calmly. "You must be used to having people around you and in two days you'd be bored out of your skull." He shrugged. "If you want to be left alone, then you need a minder to make sure the hyenas don't get you. I'd fit in well, as I'm quiet and house-trained and fairly respectable."

"I have been here for nearly a week and I am far from being bored with my own company." What he suggested was an echo of Vincent's possessiveness. She buttered another croissant and wondered why she was extending her breakfast. "Also, I am not alone all the time. I have friends here."

"You had dinner with these friends last night?"

"That's right, and tonight I repay their kindness and take them out to dinner."

"And tomorrow?"

"Who knows what they will plan?"

He made an impatient gesture. "What are you doing today?"

"I plan to spend at least four hours in the Museum of Costume."

"Christ! Four hours? With the sun shining outside?"

"I shall be engrossed and not notice that."

"Is there nothing else to do in this God-awful town?"

Penny was shocked. "It's wonderful. I have to fit as much as I can in two weeks but I shall have to leave a lot until next time I come here."

"My folks made me promise to take in Bath and Wells and Glastonbury so I'm here long enough to get the picture and send some cards, but what do I want with a heap of crumbling stones and old churches?" He leaned forward. "Have you seen the Roman bits? It's a load of ancient crap, and the spa water is enough to give you a dose of enteritis."

Penny shook her head. "Why stay here? Surely England has something to offer you without you having to insult one of our loveliest cities?"

He looked serious. "I saw you; that's why I stayed."

"Rubbish! And I'm sure you don't hate Bath as much as you say. The croissants are good and you enjoyed the park . . . and my fizzy drink. What else?"

"I had tea in the Pump Rooms and they had the best scones I've eaten outside New Zealand."

"Scones? Scones are the high point in your stay here?" Penny laughed and the waitress looked on with envy as she saw the ice melting.

"Do you make good scones? My mother makes the best scones in Rotorua."

"Bully for her! I wouldn't know where to begin!"

"You could learn."

"Would I want to do that?"

"Yes. All women make scones and Pavlovas where I come from."

"Remind me to cross New Zealand off my itinerary," she said lightly, and began to gather her belongings together.

Jake reached over and took her hand in his. "Have lunch with me," he begged. "Meet me by the river where they hire out boats and I can row us along to eat in a pub across the waterway."

She drew her hand away but hesitated. He was attractive and his touch had made her feel as if she was a real woman. It would be safe on the water and eating in a crowded pub and she had to eat somewhere.

"All right. I'll be there at one, if I don't forget the time," she said. "I may have to go back to the museum if I don't take all my notes this morning."

"Promise I'll bring you back here whenever you say, ma'am," and his smile was almost sincere.

Penny walked up to the museum, relieved to find that there was no great crowd waiting for admission, and she was soon absorbed in the beauty of the costumes, thinking again that fashion came and went full circle, with adaptations to fit in with the social climate of each era. Skirts billowed or shrank, with low necklines and diaphanous fabrics, hemlines wavered and swept the ground, with exaggerated bustles and tortured waistlines, and, much later, brushed the knee, giving a clean slim line with flat breasts and pale stockings, as different erogenous zones were considered enticing.

She frowned at the example chosen for the fashion of a few years earlier. It was one of the concoctions of leather and glitter seen on the catwalk but never in the High Street, and in her opinion not representative of the time or inclination of the women expected to wear it. As for the puff-ball skirt, ugly to wear and impossible to discipline in a taxi, it made her laugh. She had worn one just once, and decided that a charity shop was the right place for it, if anyone would buy it.

"You like that?" He saw her smiling, not with approval but with genuine amusement.

Her smile faded. "Hallo," she said and made a note on her pad as if completely absorbed.

"You work, even on holiday," Helmut said approvingly.

"Not work, just interest," she said dismissively and moved along to the safe restrictions of Victoriana.

"That is good," he said, eyeing the small waist and flowing ecru silk lace on the wax girl in the showcase. "Pretty, but so sad for women to be strapped in so tightly. That one is better, pretty, but she could breathe. That came later, with more independence for women in many ways."

"You know about costume?" Her interest was stirred.

"A little," he admitted.

"Professionally?"

"I think that you do not want to talk about your work?"

"Sorry. You mean that you don't want to talk about what you do? I didn't mean to be nosy," she said. It was ironic that she had tried to hide herself away from people on holiday and yet she was now guilty of prying into his life and found that she really wanted to know.

His smile transformed his face. "I can talk shop all day, but Gertrude told me what you do and that you are taking time away from work and people."

"Gertrude said that?"

"She . . . what do you say? She warned me away when I asked too much about you last night." He raised his shoulders in an almost Gallic way and looked apologetic.

"You saw the costumes yesterday," she accused.

"But you did not, so I knew you would be here today. We drove you away but you wanted to come here, so I knew I'd see you here, today or tomorrow."

"I see," she said weakly. "So you know I design clothes but Gertrude hasn't told me about *you*."

"I researched the costumes used in the last History of Art series, where they used set tableaux as companions to famous pictures."

"I saw all of the series. They were magnificent!"

He blushed. "I think it worked," he said modestly.

"And now?"

"I write about it and illustrate some pages." He took her notepad. "You will remember better like this."

A few quick lines showed the main features of the ecru lace and tight corseting, then he turned back the pages and saw Penny's sketches. "I apologise. You do your own very well. What a pity."

"Why?"

"You do not need me." He handed back the notepad and pen and she noticed that today he wasn't using the aftershave that Vincent favoured, and his hands were strong and smooth. A craftsman's hands, she thought.

"That one is very good and if I note the colours, I shall remember."

"You are being kind."

"Not at all." She sounded formal and glanced at her watch.

"You have an engagement?" His disappointment showed.

"I am meeting someone for lunch." Her expression softened. "I expect you are joining your parents."

"Not today. I put them on a coach for a place called Wookey Hole where they have witches." He laughed. "My stepmother will be quite at home there."

Penny giggled. "I didn't think that Germans had a sense of humour."

"I am half English and my mother was a funny lady before she became so ill. My father lost the need for humour and feels safe married to the nurse. Together they are completely German and I am not really a good fit with them. My work takes me to many places and it is good to be independent, as you have found too I think."

She nodded and wished that she was not literally pushing out the boat with Jake. "I have to go now. I am having dinner with Gertrude and Lars tonight but you could join us for coffee later, at about nine thirty?"

"I would like that, but not at the hotel, please."

A conspiratorial glance made her smile and she told him where to find them at the restaurant after dinner.

"Ah, well, at least neither of them are bores," she murmured as she walked down to the riverside. "Here today, gone tomorrow and goodbye to both of them." She wondered what Gertrude would say when she told her that she had dates with both of the men she had sworn not to encourage; but surely Lars would appreciate a few phrases for his collection, like . . . ships that pass in the night . . . and . . . safety in numbers?

Four

J ake was talking eagerly to a boatman and Penny watched them for a minute before he saw her and waved. With an animated expression, he looked boyish and very good-looking, like a student she once knew who was offered a trip in a car too valuable for him to afford. She saw that the boatman had given him a handful of leaflets and she hoped that Jake hadn't booked a more ambitious trip than he'd promised.

"Great! You're early," he said, and led her to a line of moored boats that bumped the bank of the river and then slewed round under the wake of a passing motor boat. There were canoes, which looked very unsafe when other boats rocked them, skiffs with two sets of oars, which seemed like hard work for anyone training for the Oxford and Cambridge boat race, and old-fashioned broad-based boats. Penny pointed to them and Jake chose a conventional rowing boat that had a usable footboard and two workable rowlocks. It had a carved rear seat well padded with a bright frilled cushion, and the name *Aurora* painted in red and silver curly lettering on the backrest.

She giggled. "All I need is a long skirt, a flowery hat and a parasol of lavender silk."

"Not a lot of speed, I reckon," Jake said. "But I suppose they haven't caught up with modern boats in this place. Sure you don't want a skiff?" She shook her head. "At least you'll be comfortable. No man could expect a girl to row in this hulk."

"Quite right. I shall trail a hand languidly in the water while you sweat at the oars. And I think she's lovely."

"You have to steer. Take hold of the ropes and do as I say."

"I *have* been in one or two like this before now and I do know about boats," she pointed out.

"You like the water?"

She nodded cautiously.

"Great! Tomorrow we can go white-water rafting. The guy in charge of the skiffs said there's a base a few miles away from here with all the gear." He saw her horrified expression. "You've never done it? You'll love it."

"I've never done it and I'd hate it. I do know boats, but only cabin cruisers in the Solent and dinghies on a river in Devon; no inflatables of doubtful buoyancy on angry rapids. Tomorrow I have other plans, but now I'm hungry, so cast off and let's get going."

He gave her a look filled with disbelief, as if she really must be joking, but pulled clear of the bank and started to row, while Penny steered the boat to midstream. She noticed that he had dressed with care, in spotless white jeans and a new cotton shirt with bright stripes. His trainers were well scrubbed, his face glowed with a fresh-from-the-shower cleanliness and his hair was trying to free itself from the gel that he'd applied liberally to tame it.

He rowed with nonchalant ease and the water made peaceful gurgling sounds under the hull. Penny closed her eyes, momentarily dazzled by the sun, then half opened them to look up as they passed through shade cast by the rank of weeping willows, now dangerously too close to the bank for comfort. She found her dark glasses, which were more comfortable and safer for steering.

"Pity," Jake said. "You'll take them off when we get ashore, I hope."

"I'll what?" She looked amused.

"Your shades, of course. What did you think I meant?" He grinned, and she was reminded of a delighted boy caught out telling a mildly *double entendre* joke.

"Dib dib dib," she murmured.

"What did you say?"

"Nothing. Suddenly you reminded me of a Boy Scout I once knew. Is that the restaurant over there?"

They made for the cluster of fringed sun umbrellas over white plastic tables, and tied up by a wooden landing stage. Jake jumped ashore and held out a hand for Penny. He pulled her clear, with far more force than was necessary and she found herself held closely to his stripy shirt. The smell of soap and maleness was far from unpleasant and she knew that he wanted to kiss her.

"Down boy," she said and laughed. Who had once told her that men are put off by laughter when they get heavy? Either put off or made mad, someone else had said, but Jake found it deflating.

"D'you want to sit in the sun?"

"Yes. I've got a hat and sunglasses."

"We'll sit in the shade and you can look pretty," he said firmly. "I've seen better hats on a donkey."

"Funny you should say that. My boyfriend hates it, too."

"He should know better than to let you off the leash alone, even with the hat." He inspected her left hand. "Boyfriend? At least you aren't married." In his mind, Vincent melted away as an inconvenience and no more. "Where is he?"

"America," Penny said, but couldn't put on a sad face. Vincent seemed far away in time and miles and no way would he have suggested rowing a hired boat or lazing on the river, unless it was in a punt poled by someone else, with Vincent in a straw boater and striped waistcoat, hoping to be recognised by someone important in the theatre, and preferably with a hamper of smoked salmon and champagne in the stern.

"Good. Do you like whitebait?" He studied the menu and seemed puzzled. "How do they serve them? It says with brown bread and butter and lemon. We have them in fritters at home."

"You can't put fat little fishes in fritters. They are fried crisp and brown and are eaten with a fork. Look over there. The man in the baseball cap is eating them."

Jake strolled over and stared at the small fish. The man looked up at him. "Something troubling you?"

"That's whitebait?"

"Any objection?"

"Back home they are small and like little worms." Jake grinned. "These look better. Don't mind if I try some. Thanks, mate. No, I'm not trying to be funny, I'm not from round here and I really wanted to know."

"He thought you wanted to help yourself to his," giggled Penny. "It's a nasty habit *I'd* noticed."

He looked wounded. "I only *looked*. Ours at home are transparent before they're cooked and look like threads of silk," he told Penny. "I never thought they tasted of anything but salt water and batter, but those are like tiny sprats and smell good."

"So you'll remember some good things about Bath. I'll have them too and a half of Guinness."

"Girls drink beer in England?"

"Of course, and I usually drink Guinness with pub food."

"Do you ever drink in pubs at night alone or with another girl?"

"If I'm thirsty or there's an entertainment or a poetry reading that isn't sheer crap. There are a lot of readings in pubs and some are really good." Even Vincent wasn't above taking part if he thought it would be noticed.

"Don't you get, well aren't men a bit . . . ?"

"You mean that men try to pick up women in pubs?"

"Well, don't they?"

"Single women wouldn't do much if they had to have a man with them at all times." Penny tried to sound patient. "Some men try to get acquainted but it's easy to give them the elbow if they get stroppy, and we have as much right to a quiet drink as they have, so where's the problem?" She smiled. "I have a few very pungent phrases in French and Italian and one Anglo-Saxon one that usually sends them packing, but there isn't a lot of hassle."

"Glad I escaped, but you weren't exactly friendly. Maybe you liked me," he said hopefully. "I can't believe that you really do go to pubs alone. You don't feel threatened? You really do drink in pubs alone?"

"This is *now*, Jake, not before World War Two when women were much less free. War-time service and the absence of men altered that a lot. I've heard strange things about Kiwis and Aussies but you're the first one I've met fresh from down under. Now I think I believe at least half of what I've been told."

"What have you heard?"

She laughed. "Eat up your whitebait. It's hot but it needs to be eaten at once or it loses its crispness." She filled her mouth so that she couldn't speak and after a long hard look at her, he did the same.

Penny eyed him with amusement at his apparent worry that the reputation of his entire country depended on her opinion.

"Now tell me," he insisted when they were drinking coffee. "What lies have you heard about Kiwi men?"

She appeared to give the matter serious consideration. "Women in New Zealand do not drink alone in pubs or whatever you have that ranks as a pub there, or so I'm told?"

"Correct. Only women on the make do that and they're asking for trouble."

"In fact, women do not go to bars even with their menfolk?" She looked amused and incredulous.

"Not to bars." He seemed censorious. "They go out for meals in cafés and restaurants with their men," he added hastily, "but not bars. They are for men and men like to keep it that way and women wouldn't like it."

"How do you know? Are they ever invited?"

He ignored her remark. "Bars over there are just that. Bars are high tables where men stand and drink, not like pubs here with small tables and chairs and bar stools up at a counter, and food . . . and liberated women who risk being harassed."

"So what do the women do when the men are drinking?"

He looked embarrassed. "Stay at home or visit girlfriends, I guess. Look after the kids."

"And bake scones?" She was laughing now. "You have to be joking. There must be thousands of professional women out there who can't take that sort of life."

"It comes naturally if they are born there and they love it. They have interesting jobs and friends, and clubs for women, so they don't need men to fill their evenings – unless they have a barbie," he added. "New Zealand is a young out-of-doors culture and we swim and sail and raft and fish a lot. The women join in sometimes, if they want to. It's a wonderful country and I know you'd love it, Penny."

"I design clothes and I mix with a lot of theatrefolk and some quite intelligent people who paint or write and love history. The buildings here in Bath take away my breath." She eyed him with curiosity. "What would I do there? I'm not drawn to any of the very male pursuits you mention and I couldn't put a worm on a hook or take a fish off to save my life."

"*We* have history, if you like that sort of thing."

"Going back a couple of hundred years?"

"I'm sure it's longer, but I'm not into all that." He sounded impatient. "We like things to be functional. We pull down anything that gets tatty and put up new modern buildings, although more old buildings are being preserved as a kind of novelty for the tourists." He saw she was unimpressed. "There's a fine set of really old buildings in Rotorua and an old-fashioned bowling green where the women wear white gear and hats to match. Really weird," he added. "We do have an ancient Maori culture that goes back and back."

"Now that I would like to see."

"Come back with me and I'll show it to you."

"Don't be silly. We've been together for a few hours and I suspect that you are on your best behaviour. I know nothing about you. What do you do apart from fishing and bungee jumping?"

He blushed as he sensed her inner laughter. "I went to agricultural college and I work on the family sheep farm. I have my own house now and oversee a lot of land and about five thousand sheep, or I will do when I get back from my holiday. I needed a break after college and this is my reward for doing well."

"Family?"

"Mother and Father are almost retired and live in a smaller farmhouse in South Island, and they have an apartment in Rotorua in North Island. My elder brother is in overall charge and has the original house with his wife and three children."

"What do you do in the evenings?"

"Evenings? Nobody stays up late as it's an early start."

"You mean you often stay up until nine o'clock?" Her raised eyebrows were eloquent.

"Shut up will ya? You don't understand."

44

"You go to bed that early? What if you are a night owl and not a lark? What about parties?"

"We have barbies at weekends at lunchtime that go on into the evening and a good night or two when the shearers are there."

"The women must enjoy that." There was no hiding her sarcasm. "A real excuse for dressing up and dancing the night away."

"The women don't go there, and they don't dress up. It gets a bit rough and the shearers have a reputation for the amount of beer they can hold."

"They just cook for them?"

"Yes." He sounded relieved. "They enjoy doing that. They get together, enjoy each other's company and have a laugh or two, and we have a good spread." He saw her shake her head. "They really do enjoy it. More coffee?"

"Please. I think I need some extra caffeine."

"We have fine scenery and a lot of volcanoes and mud pools," he said defensively. "Do you like mountains?"

"Some."

"Thank God for that. We have mountains and nature reserves." She nodded and he was encouraged. "Hot pools to sit in and a lot of thermal energy."

"I'm sure you love it because you were brought up in New Zealand, but I must have lovely buildings and culture and good clothes."

"You don't know what you're missing."

"I'm beginning to think I do know," she said gently. "I see a cloud up there and I ought to get back."

"You've plenty of time before your dinner date."

"Not really. I have some shopping to do and I do like to dress up a little as a compliment to my friends, who I know will take trouble to look very good."

"Vanity."

"No, just good manners in this country and in some other old countries of Europe."

She recollected a French chateau, now an elegant and expensive hotel, where she stayed with friends after a dress show in Switzerland. A tactful but forceful notice in the bedrooms said in four languages that the proprietors were sure that guests would appreciate the ambience of the ancient castle and the trouble the staff took for their comfort; and as the food was of exquisite quality and variety and cooked with expertise, gentlemen would obviously wish to do it justice and respect the quality of the dining-room by making each meal a celebration and wearing suitable clothes and ties. If guests wished to be more informal dinner would be served in the guest rooms or suites.

It had been a relief to see men dressed with care and not sitting in sloppy, though expensive, garments more suitable for the gymnasium than for the celebration of gourmet food.

"Let's go." He seemed to give up and looked unhappy. She followed him to the moored boat. "You seem to be a bit of a women's libber. You can row back."

"Thought you'd never suggest it," she said happily, and slid into the seat and adjusted the rowlocks. He watched her ease between two badly moored boats and find open water. Her eyes were shining and she wondered why she had not kept up her rivercraft in London or at least in Surrey, where she had rowed on fine summer evenings with a carefree crowd before Vincent came along.

"You were telling lies," he said. "You do like outdoor sports."

"I like sticky jam doughnuts but only once a year. This is a treat but I'd get fed up if it was all there was on offer."

"You know I'm crazy about you?"

"No!"

"Yes, and if I could get you home with me, you'd fall in love with the country." She looked away from the hunger in his face and was glad that a boat nearly rammed them from the side, making her swerve and row faster. "Time is against me I know, and so I have to say it now and not lead up to it gently. I fell in love in the park and I've looked round every corner here since then, hoping to see you, and today has been wonderful."

"I've enjoyed it too."

"Row over there under the willows. We need to talk, Penny."

"I can hear you from here. I've been in the shade for long enough and I want the sun on my back."

"Spoilsport." He grinned in defeat and her pulse quickened. She almost did pull in behind the veil of weeping willows, but decided that it might be more than she wanted just now.

She rowed on in silence, aware of him and the fact that her shirt was taut as she bent to the oars.

Jake regarded her with approval and twice announced that he loved her, as if to brainwash her into accepting it.

"Make fast," she called, as if she had heard nothing of importance. The boat brushed the bank and she shipped her oars trimly.

Once more, he gripped her hand to help her to land, but this time he kissed her, with lips that smelled of coffee and ice-cream but thankfully not of fish, and his kiss was hard and desperate.

"Friends," Penny said and kissed his cheek. "Just good friends."

"No. I want you, Penny. Just to touch you makes me know this is real."

"You haven't thought this through. Think of what we said at lunch and see what real barriers there are. We come from completely different backgrounds and I have many commitments to my work, people who are employed in the workshop and cutting room, and you have to go back to your farm. Physical attraction isn't enough and I don't have one-night stands with anyone. It doesn't work out."

"You've tried that?" He looked horrified.

"Yes, and I had a lover for over two years. Don't look so shocked. You must have had girls?"

"That's different. Men have to get experience."

"Men *are* different and I think Kiwis are even more different. Rather old-fashioned and chauvinistic in fact. Goodbye, Jake, and thank you for a lovely outing."

"When do I see you again?"

"I have no idea." She saw that he was really unhappy.

"I might go round the Roman Baths tomorrow. Want to come?"

"Oh, *no*! I don't think I could bear it."

"Fine. You go rafting and I'll browse through history."

"The day after?"

"The Costume Museum again, or perhaps the American Museum. You might like that. Real ginger biscuits and maybe scones. I think a quiche or two for lunch with lots of salad but it's ages since I was there and we didn't stay to see everything as Vincent didn't enjoy it much." She frowned. "I can't recall where we did have lunch. It might have been in a café outside the museum. I know I wanted to go back to see it all in detail but I never managed to return until now."

"I'll take you there in the morning," Jake said firmly.

She teased him a little. "Just your style. The women dress in pinafores and mob-caps and cook all day for their menfolk, to show how they lived in covered-wagon days in America. They also made quilts during the long winter evenings. Women knew their place in the bad old days."

"They still do where I come from, or they did, but I admit that things are changing and men and women are partners more often now." He jutted his chin. "But the man must be the boss."

"I don't believe it. You think they are but there's an art in seeming to be docile and yet getting your own way in important matters. I'm not too good at it as yet but I learned a lot in the last two years and I found that my independence is far too precious ever to be in thrall to a man again." She shrugged. "Some girls can combine the two and are very, very good at getting just what they want without losing their femininity."

"If you came back with me, you could have whatever you wanted, so long as you wanted me. You could set up in business there."

She shook her head. "I have too many people who depend on me for a living, and I like England."

"Don't you ever travel to get new ideas?"

"Of course, but I hadn't considered New Zealand or Australia. I never use Kiwi feathers," she said solemnly.

"You should come with me, we have Maori designs and we mine pure jade for jewellery in every colour from pale cream to black with the real green jade colour in between."

"Sounds fine."

"Do you really have a dinner date tonight with the Swedish couple?"

"Of course I have. I may even have business contacts with Gertrude when I get home."

"What does he do?"

"He sees to the financial side of her very successful business, the taxes and investments, and they travel together. He gave up his job to do so," she said, and smiled. "Some men are happy to work with their wives."

"And she's the boss?" He whistled softly. "Christ! He must be a weirdo."

"Not at all. They depend on each other and they are in love."

"Can I see you later, after dinner?"

"No." Penny felt mildly embarrassed and wondered what Jake would say if she told him that Helmut was to join the party after dinner for coffee. "I think Gertrude has invited someone from their tour group," she said.

"Good. You can leave them and come out with me. There must be a nightclub somewhere even if we have to wear Roman togas," he said scathingly.

"Not my scene." She smiled and touched his arm. "Sorry Jake, nothing more today. See you at ten, the day after tomorrow, at the bus stop by the bridge."

"It will have to be a bus or a taxi. I have no car here, but if I stay longer I shall hire one."

"Very wise. A car in Bath can be a nightmare with such limited parking unless your hotel has a car-park, which is very rare. Bath was built for carriages and horsemen and had no lines of parked vehicles on every kerb in Regency times."

"Come touring with me, Penny? We can go to Scotland and the Lake District."

"I love the sea but I'm not so keen on lakes. Too static and a bit daunting, as I always think they're bottomless. A bit sinister unless water flows and has waves and can take a sailing boat."

"Some of the lakes back home are huge and can get very rough. They are deep of course, where they have been formed by volcanic eruptions, but the sailing is wonderful and the fishing is great."

"I've seen the pictures," she said gently. "I'm sure it's everything you say, but I can't imagine myself there for a long time ahead. I have work to do."

"I'll walk you home."

"No, Jake. I want to do some shopping and you must book up for your rafting before the places are all taken by eager Japs and Germans."

"Too right! See you at the bus stop."

"Goodbye." She watched him go and tried to think of her shopping and forget the set of his shoulders and the tight-fitting trousers. Sex! What had Gertrude said? There was a danger of taking another lover just to fill a gap left by Vincent, a gap that could be filled with someone . . . or just anyone, not at all what she really needed.

The fabrics in Milsom Street were too good to pass and she bought several lengths of ethnic prints and some dark soft woollens. The shop would send them to the studio and Josie could look at them and see if they gave her any ideas.

An old pharmacy selling gentle scents and soaps that Penny remembered from her childhood was doing a good trade with Americans who liked the idea of lavender-scented linen cupboards just like Grandma had in the past, and unfounded memories of English cottage gardens that were to them folk history, half believed.

Impulsively, Penny bought rose scent and lavender soap for Aunt Monica and a pretty gingham tea cosy that she knew her aunt would like. She had a feeling that Jake would expect to pay for everything when they were together, as "going Dutch" would not appeal to him, so she bought more of the same and had it packaged separately so that he could take it to his mother.

Five

The evening sun made the stones warm and the figures on the façade of the Abbey less harsh than they appeared in bleak weather; and stalls selling drinks and snacks were doing a roaring trade. Two students made a valiant attempt to convince the watching crowds that they were skilled jugglers and a girl, dressed in one of Oxfam's long and voluminous skirts and a brilliant ethnic shirt, whispered a song to the twang of a zither.

The precincts of the Abbey throbbed with the music and the sound of people talking in many languages and the remorseless click of camera shutters as Japanese took pictures of everything that moved and most of what stayed put on the walls of the Abbey.

Penny was early and sat on a bench, enjoying the warmth and the spectacle around her. Tomorrow was fully taken with more costumes, then the Roman Baths and the history of Sulis and Minerva, and then the day after, Jake again and the American Museum. He had made no mention of how long he intended to stay in Bath but she had a shrewd suspicion that it depended on her reaction to his company. He no longer said anything about going home after he left Bath, but surely he must get back to take up his new job.

She walked across to drop a few coins into the gaping baseball cap that was set on the ground to accept contributions to Art, and avoided a man pushing militant literature

52

into the hands of the mostly foreign visitors, who couldn't read the message but took the pamphlets for souvenirs. She then walked to the restaurant to wait for Gertrude and Lars, feeling that she was about to greet real friends.

They were there before her, drinking Pernod in the small bar, and Lars came forward as soon as he saw her at the door, bringing her to Gertrude and asking what she would like to drink. He had put on a well-cut natural linen jacket and pale blue linen trousers and shirt, a pale tie, and his tan shoes shone like polished chestnuts.

"You do look nice," Penny said and smiled mischievously. "Gertrude doesn't look bad either!"

Gertrude inclined her head graciously. "I think at times that Lars wants to tread the catwalk. Have you a contact for him, Penny?" She spread the soft pleats of her cream silk skirt and crossed her elegant legs to show the finely cut-away slender-heeled sandals, and Penny was glad that she had made an effort to dress well too. She laughed softly, and Gertrude raised her eyebrows. "We are funny?"

"No, you both look marvellous. I was thinking of what Jake told me today. I'm afraid you wouldn't do for his world in New Zealand unless you were going to a wedding. Don't you possess denim shorts and sandals?"

"They are primitives in New Zealand? Savages?" asked Lars.

"No, just so very laid back, they are almost supine . . . on their backs!" He looked puzzled. "I mean casual in their way of dressing," Penny rephrased, remembering that Lars had a very good working knowledge of English but certain terms escaped him. His face cleared and she could almost hear the cogs in his brain putting the new phrase into its slot.

"You and Jake were together?"

"We rowed on the river in a very old-fashioned boat with dodgy rowlocks and had a pub lunch."

"And were you both . . . laid back very far?" he asked with an air of false innocence.

"We enjoyed the outing, but I kept my feet firmly on the ground," Penny answered him. "I am going to the American Museum with him the day after tomorrow but I have already refused an invitation to go back with him to New Zealand."

"He has progressed so far?"

"I have a feeling that he acts on impulse and he might manage to marry a girl in between shearing a few hundred sheep." Her tone was wry and she felt that she could see Jake more clearly now that she was away from him and with sensible friends.

"Do you never act on impulse?" Gertrude asked solemnly.

"Sometimes," she admitted. "But I hope I've learned to take a little time to consider what comes next. I moved in with Vincent on the whim that we suited each other. I was fond of him and I was far too busy and lazy to leave him until we had the final scene and he went to America. Everyone believed we were a permanent pair and he scared off a lot of casual lechers."

Without Vincent's frowning influence she had very nearly gone into the privacy of the overhanging willows with Jake, but she didn't think it necessary to say anything about that.

The waiter handed them menus to consider over their drinks and Penny felt hungry as she realised she had eaten nothing but the whitebait all day.

"Fruit to start a meal?" Lars frowned. "Is it pears or peaches? It says Mendip wall fruit and I think that peaches grow on walls."

Penny giggled. "Someone has an odd sense of humour, just to puzzle the visitors, but even some local people don't know what it means. It's the same as escargots, you know, snails in garlic butter."

"They come from the Mendip Hills? We saw no snails today in Cheddar and Wells."

"They say that the Romans brought them to England and descendants of the same species with stripy shells are farmed on Mendip now."

"I will try," Lars said. "I am impressed by the food in English restaurants here. We ate good gravlax and smoked salmon the other day."

"Not typical English food," Penny pointed out. "But they have to keep the Swedes happy, and a rash of seaweed has infected Bath to please the Japs." They were shown to their table and ate in a leisurely manner, finding out more about each other and liking what they heard.

As Penny described Vincent in more detail she realised just how selfish he was and how much she had given in to his wishes.

"Have you heard from him?"

"A picture card from Boston and one from New York, more to impress me than to tell me any news. I shall hear nothing once he's busy."

"Perhaps he will write when he needs you," Gertrude guessed shrewdly.

"I hope not. Vincent can be very pathetic if things go wrong, and I have been his main prop, I suppose."

"But now you are free and he will find another woman?"

"I hope he will." :

"You hope? You are not sure?"

"I'm sure he could, but he's used to me and might think he could pick up where we left off. I do have a conscience about him. He was useful in all sorts of ways and I was happy for a time."

"Don't look back or make a lot of anguish for yourself. He is doing what suits him." Gertrude was firm. "If you go to bed with Jake, and tell Vincent that you have a new lover, that should settle him for good. He sounds a vain man who would not want you after that."

"Jake will go away, and I don't have casual sex."

"No." Gertrude smiled. "He would be a charming lover but not for you. Also, he would want to take you for ever and that is not as I think and as you say . . . on the cards?"

Lars sighed. "Have some fruit and ice-cream and stop being a witch," he said.

"Helmut said he had sent his father and stepmother to Wookey Hole where they say there are witches. He was evidently very annoyed with her and said she would fit in well there."

"You have been busy. You talked to Helmut?"

"Briefly. He found me in the Costume Museum and I think he had been looking for me."

"When do you see him again?"

"I hope you don't mind? I invited him for coffee after dinner tonight. He will join us for coffee here and not at the hotel where Frau Braun might be waiting for him. I hope you have no objection. It was the easiest way to get rid of him."

Lars went to the men's room and came back with Helmut who had been lurking in the bar until he thought it late enough to venture in to join them. They left the table and ordered coffee in the lounge.

Gertrude eyed his tobacco brown cotton suit and knitted tie with approval and noticed that the soft plaited belt that encircled his waist was an expensive item. "Good leather," she remarked.

"It is deerskin and I think from abroad, probably North American Indian where they have a lot of deer."

"Or New Zealand," Gertrude said with a wicked smile. "Penny was telling us that deer are farmed there."

"You have been there?" His interest was genuine, and he seemed disappointed when Penny shook her head. "I wish to go there to sketch the Maori carvings, and to attend a Hangi feast. A friend wants to put on ethnic shows and a Maori backdrop would be impressive. I have the music and we know people from Christchurch University who will help us." He named a famous television show that dealt with ancient cultures and histories of far-off lands.

"I saw the programme about Peru," Penny said. "The handwoven fabrics were superb, and we used similar themes for a spring show."

"I may be sent out to Australia and New Zealand soon," Helmut said, and looked pleased. "You should go there and see what the true Maoris wear, and how they live."

"I know little about the country or anyone who lives there."

"You would know me," he said calmly. "I would look after you." She looked away from his intent gaze. Suddenly, she wanted to giggle and tried to hide the amusement that made her lips twitch. Two men on the same day wanted her to go to New Zealand with them, to very different separate venues. Sheep and barbies, or academia and a seat of learning of which Jake had given her no hint.

"It could be on the cards," Gertrude said mildly. "What do you say, a possibility?" She was enjoying Penny's confusion. "Suddenly you might find that New Zealand was full of people you know."

"Small world," Penny murmured.

"It is fashionable to go there," Helmut agreed, "but more young people are travelling in Europe now and some stay to work here."

"Not the sheep farmers."

Penny gave Gertrude a warning glance and she smiled and was silent.

"Each one has his own home," Helmut agreed. "Mine is in several places. It has been in Munich where my father and stepmother live and where my mother died, but increasingly I live in London and sometimes in France."

"Never in Sweden?" Lars wanted to know. "Penny has never seen our country also. You are both missing a lot if you never visit Sweden. You must come there."

"Are you inviting us together?" His laugh was only half amused. "That would be a delight."

"For us, certainly."

"I'm not very fond of snow and cold weather," Penny said, dismissing Sweden completely and wanting to kick Lars for his efforts at bringing two people together, just because he had begun to like them very much.

"It is warm in summer," Gertrude said.

"So is France," Penny replied briskly. "I might have work to do in Paris but, so far, no one in Sweden has shown an interest in my work."

"I have." Gertrude eyed her mischievously. "I have contacts and I want to work with you on drapes and purses for a collection that would soon find favour with Sweden."

Helmut looked on, smiling, but sensed the tension behind Penny's words. "I shall take a raincheck on Sweden," he said at last. "First I need to visit New Zealand."

"Raincheck? Oh, I understand," Lars said. "You too have many strange English phrases, Helmut, and you are half German."

"Take my business card and keep it so that when you come to Sweden you may visit us," Gertrude said.

He put it carefully in his wallet and smiled. "Have you given one to Penny, also?"

"Of course."

"See you around, perhaps in Sweden," he said softly. "I like that even if it is not a promise."

"Are you going to be around? When do you and your family leave Bath?" asked Lars.

"They go the day after tomorrow but I want to stay for a few days. I shall meet them again in London where we shall stay at Brown's Hotel."

Penny said nothing of her plans to return home when Gertrude suggested meeting Helmut in London in a week's time.

"It's late and I think time to go home," Penny said lightly. "I'm full of sunshine and good food and I'm sleepy."

"I shall walk with you," Helmut said firmly, and she couldn't think why not, so she paid her bill and said her goodbyes and joined him at the front of the restaurant.

"How tired are you? It's a fine night and very warm and a walk would be good," he said.

"Great," she heard herself say and they went slowly through the Abbey square and down the steps to the river walk. Music from an upper room overlooking the weir reminded her that Jake had suggested a nightclub. She wondered if he was there, adding to the noise, and hoped that he didn't emerge just as they were passing.

Couples stood by the wall in the shadow of the bridge, closely entwined as if they feared being dragged apart from each other, and other couples on the grass seemed very fully occupied. Penny chose to ignore them and walked along the lighted path.

"Who begins?" His smile was sweet and his voice gentle and amused.

"Who begins what?"

"We have to get to know each other and I shall tell you my whole life history unless you stop me."

"I know enough. You have a degree in history and a

diploma in costume design and several awards for work in the theatre and television and you love old buildings. I have seen that you are very talented as I have one of your illustrations. Isn't that enough?"

"No. You know nothing of me, the person."

"I know what I see, Helmut. I see a man who I would like to have as a friend. I feel sure that he is not a criminal or a violent man but is someone I can trust." She glanced at his face. "A little sad perhaps, but kind."

"All true, but you do not ask if I am married or about to be married and if I have had a little experience of love?" His hand rested lightly on her arm and for a moment she was intensely aware of him. "I would like you to be curious about that, as it could concern you."

"Well, are you married?"

"No, and I have no mistress."

She smiled at the old-fashioned word but her voice was unsteady. "I lived with a man for two years and he wanted me to follow him to America." Vincent, who had been so useless in many ways, was now an excuse, a barrier behind which she could hide when a man showed sexual interest in her. Wryly, she knew that he would be flattered and believe that she really loved him and could bear no other man to take her to bed!

"My English is not perfect, but you spoke in the past tense." His arm rested on her shoulders and she felt the warmth of his body and the uneasy safety of his touch.

"We parted for ever before I came away," she admitted. "I have a lot of things to decide, and I needed time and peace in which to do it."

"Do you love him?"

"Two years together leaves a lot to remember and I am still fond of him," she finished weakly.

"As I am of my Old English sheepdog," he replied

gravely. "I have had him for four years but I left him in Germany as he would not be happy in quarantine. I am fond of him, but I do not weep that I can have him with me no longer. He will be happy with my father and be of use, making him walk and keep thin."

Penny laughed. "Vincent would be very annoyed to be compared to a dog!"

"Please do not go to America," he said simply. "Come, it is late and you need to sleep."

His arm had slid from her shoulder and they walked in silence until she stopped at her front door. "May I call for you tomorrow night for dinner? Please," he added with sudden vehemence. "We have many things to discuss. We enjoy the same things and we could become close friends."

"About eight?"

"Bless you." He put out a hand, then drew back and didn't touch her. "Good-night, bright Penny."

"So you did know about British coins," she said, and laughed. "You are dishonest! I thought that you were just another ignorant tourist who hadn't done his homework."

"It was better to hold your hand and have a lesson in counting out the right money."

"Come in and have more coffee," she suggested. An inner voice warned her that she was again acting on impulse and that coffee might grow cold if he came closer.

Helmut leaned forward and kissed her gently on the lips. "If I did, I would want to make love to you. Go to bed and stop looking like that."

He turned away and she watched him stride to the corner of the street and disappear without looking back.

"Well, I need more coffee, even if he doesn't." She was resentful and embarrassed and felt cheap. Did he think she was propositioning him? Her hands were trembling when she poured the coffee. I'll have to sort out my feelings. I'm raw and, as Gertrude said, vulnerable. What happened to the planned peaceful nun-like existence in a busy tourist city? How did I get two men . . . breathing down my neck? She smiled. Lars now knew what that meant and would use the phrase when he had a captive audience ready to listen to his new English.

She stripped and turned on the shower. She felt heavy and bad-tempered and found that her period had begun. The warm water streamed down her face and drenched her hair, caressed her body and released her tension. It was like the sudden appearance of a strict nanny, forbidding any kind of sexual activity until she had gone away again.

When Vincent was with her, Penny had used the Pill as he could not be relied on. His attempts with condoms were so laughable that it robbed sex of any romance, and they usually abandoned the effort with her in giggles and Vincent stony-faced and offended.

Smelling sweetly of Country Garden talc and soap, she put on a clean cotton nightie and sat in bed trying to concentrate on her book. But reading was difficult as the "What ifs" spiralled in her brain.

What if Helmut had tried to make love to her? Would he have coldly planned a seduction and come prepared with protection? Did he refuse her invitation to coffee knowing that it would lead to sex and he was *not* prepared? Was it likely that men would carry protection at all times? She laughed softly. How embarrassing for him to say words to the effect of "I just happened to have this with me, in case!" If Jake took her to bed would he bother, or were all women in New Zealand on the Pill and ready for any emergency or the chance that men might condescend to fancy them?

She put out the light and snuggled down on the hard mattress, tucking an extra pillow behind her back to be comfortable. It was like beginning again, the advent of maturity. Her mother had said severely when her first period came, "Now he careful! If you let a boy do things to you, you will have a baby and I have no intention of bringing up grandchildren! One generation was enough."

It was said in a relaxed way but the message was clear and for Penny sex was a forbidden and little-discussed avenue until she went to university. She was advised to take the Pill by a tutor who knew all about the sudden rush of testosterone and adrenalin that could happen in dark corners on warm evenings, but Penny had refused, having doubts about its safety, and was lucky that the first time she had casual sex, more out of curiosity than passion, the more experienced man took precautions and it was only when Vincent proved so ham-handed that she took her own.

She slept and woke curiously refreshed and happy. I have control of my body and my own future. I can say no to all men unless I choose to change my mind. In a way I am protected against my own impulses as I'd not dare to make love now. She wondered how many women could use her excuse to refuse sex or were most brainwashed into thinking they must be available and so had to be protected for their own sakes?

The dress she chose was almost a caftan with soft pleats from the shoulder and good bright colours to offset her pallor. She popped a tube of mild pain-killers into her bag and hoped her backache would subside. At least she had no headaches after giving up the Pill and she looked forward to her day.

I have space, she decided. A beautiful green space that I can enjoy alone unless I choose to admit another person to share it with me. There had been few such spaces of tranquillity over the past few years and she must cherish it.

On the way to the museum, she passed the hotel where

Gertrude and Lars and Helmut were staying. Was the visit to England a green space for Helmut? She considered his past and the agony of seeing a beloved mother suffer over a long-drawn-out dying.

She hurried on. That's his problem, she told herself, but hated having to dismiss him from her mind so that she could concentrate on her research.

Six

Her eyes felt hot as she tried to sketch the costumes in a dim light and Penny decided to rest during the afternoon. She had an idea that Jake might return from his watery efforts and she didn't want to see him until tomorrow, so she went back to her apartment in case he appeared round the next corner. Bath seemed to shrink each time she ventured out.

Once again she was thankful to have an apartment to herself: being able to leave the phone off the hook if necessary was a luxury. Even the thought of seeing Gertrude wasn't what she wanted. She pulled the curtains and slept for three hours as if she was exhausted.

A cool shower and some iced coffee revived her, and she was no longer bothered by fluid retention. She flicked through her drawings and decided to send some to Josie to mull over. She found a picture card of Bath Abbey which cut down the need for a long letter to explain about the sketches and as she brushed her hair before Helmut tapped on the front door with the brass lion-head door knocker, she felt that she had spent the day wisely.

"You slept," he said.

"How did you know?"

"There is the mark of a honeycomb blanket on your arm and your eyes are bright as if you have rested them."

She blushed. "And what did you do this afternoon? I am not a detective like you, so you must tell me."

"I sat in the Abbey and thought of you."

Her reply was flippant to hide her sudden alarm. "You were supposed to think of God and the angels, not women you meet on holiday."

"One woman."

"Not all the afternoon? How boring for you."

"It was easy, but I was there for only two hours. The rest of the time I went to make sure that the travelling and hotel arrangements were complete for my father and stepmother to go to London tomorrow. I found a few events in London that I thought they should see."

"How considerate. Are you leaving Bath too? Suddenly, you know all about London and can manage British coinage?"

"You taught me well. At least I had an excuse to meet you." He grinned. "No, I'm still planning to stay. I would like to take you to Glastonbury tomorrow."

"Tomorrow I am going to the American Museum with a friend." She came to the conclusion that Helmut must not think that he was the only man available to her. She was haunted by the thought that they would all meet and she would have to explain the one to the other.

He nodded and grinned. "Gertrude told me that the New Zealander wanted to take you out."

"She did?"

"I had coffee with them and he came to speak to Gertrude, asking if they knew where you might be at five o'clock today. He didn't ask me." His smile was cool and betrayed nothing of his feelings. "He had seen you with Gertrude and thought you might be in her pocket."

"I made no plans to see him today and he wanted to see the American Museum tomorrow, so it seemed a good idea to go there together." Why am I almost apologising? She felt an anger born of guilt. Neither of them had any claim on her and she could go out with whoever she liked!

"I did not think you had been with him today. His hair and T-shirt were very wet."

Penny laughed. "White-water rafting, I believe. Not my idea of fun."

"I'm pleased to hear that. I have no desire to do it either." They walked to the restaurant in silence, then he said, "You like this Jake?"

"Very much. I have met some really, really nice people in Bath. First Gertrude and Lars, Jake, and now you." She gave him a sweet smile that did nothing for his self-esteem as Jake and he were bundled in together as passing friends.

"What does he do at home?"

"He farms sheep and has a passion for outdoor activities," she said simply.

Helmut gave an exaggerated shudder. "How very bucolic."

She laughed. "You sounded very English County."

"My mother was," he confessed and smiled more naturally.

"Then surely you know all about farming, too," she teased him.

"Not like that. I do have some land in Dorset that was my mother's but it is mostly arable farming with a few hens and cows. It's run by a manager and I have been there twice only since my mother died."

"Would you ever live there?"

"It depends." He led her to the bar. "An aperitif?"

"You are half British. Do you never feel a pull towards living here?"

"I am at home wherever my work takes me and I love travelling. If I settle down one day it must be because I can't stay away from a place or I love a person who holds me there." He raised his glass and looked at her with a quizzical smile. "Here's to Dorset. You must see it soon. You will like it."

"I do know some of it. Who hasn't stood on the mole in Lyme Bay and looked out to sea like the French Lieutenant's Woman or wondered how the Victorians kept their skirts dry when they walked along it?"

"They lifted the hems on ribbons sewn into the skirts, or they do when I interpret the design of a costume, but modern fabrics are easy to clean, not like the heavy baratheas and serge." He glanced at her sharply. "Now you think I am all German! Precise and taking everything said to me seriously and at face value."

"What's wrong with that if I really am interested?"

He sighed. "Even now I find my two sides difficult to understand. When I am in Germany, I feel like a Brit on alien soil and when I am in England I often feel foreign." He grinned. "My stepmother helps."

"She helps you? Have you all that in common?"

"That's why. I do not like her and she doesn't like me and I think my mother would have been happier with an English nurse." He shrugged. "I was away a lot and she was very efficient and convinced my father that she was indispensable, so I can have no real quarrel with her, but she makes me feel very British at times and I think I am more comfortable that way. She helps my national schizophrenia."

"So, what's the answer? To live in France or Italy where you would be foreign and comfortable trying to live with yet another language and culture, and as it was not your concern, able to be objective and not take sides?"

"Or to keep on travelling, which is self-indulgent but tempting."

"If you are lucky enough to afford it and your work takes

you to exotic places, it sounds a wonderful way to spend your life."

"It is." He grinned and she smiled in response to the charm that made him warm and very attractive. They studied the large leather-bound menus and followed the waiter into the restaurant. Penny was conscious of good silver and immaculate table linen and appreciated the difference between her life now and the mostly self-catering life as a student and struggling designer. Jake would be a student type for the rest of his life unless he married a wife who would nag him to dress well and eat in more up-market places than the traditional American-style diners he was used to.

She touched the small display of tiny roses in the silver bowl and found them cool and fresh. "Nice! I hate fake flowers."

"I can see that I can expect no sympathy from you for a poor man torn between two countries."

"Right! I think you have everything you want."

"Everything I need, but I want other things. I want you, Penny."

She sipped the cold Chablis and couldn't meet his gaze. The grilled sole suddenly needed a lot of attention and she sensed that he was waiting for her to look at him again, his silence more compelling than words.

She drank more wine and looked at him. "We all want things that may be impossible," she ventured. "I never thought I'd have much success with my designs. I was good at college, but it was only after three years that I really emerged as a recognised designer, and there are still other things I want to do, but I can't expect to have every wish granted me."

She bit her lip. "I owe something to Vincent. He was a cosy pillow that took the impact of the outside world and I could progress in my own time, in peace."

"That was what he wanted you to think, to bind you closely and convince you that you needed him for ever."

"Isn't that what we all do in different ways? Friends and lovers do depend on each other."

"Perhaps, but you have broken away completely, which shows that you don't need him now, and I believe that he will be more deprived of you than you could be of him. You were not in love, Penny."

"I am still very . . ."

"Fond of him? Woof woof!"

She took a deep breath. "Don't sneer! You don't know him and you are not being fair. You know nothing about me either, but you are crowding me. You are a man I met on holiday who I like very much and who I think fancies me a little; so does Jake, so where does that leave me? I have yet to forget my life with Vincent and I have work to do that does not include time for a passing casual affair. How many times have we met? Twice? Three times?" Her eyes were stormy. "Bath was to be a kind of oasis, a space for recovery, but I feel pressured. I am not ready to be rushed."

"I'm glad you feel pressured," he said simply. "Feel that pressure and know that I love you. Get angry because I am peeling away your comfort and the negation of your real feelings." He laughed. "Besides, I have so little time to convince you that you need me more than any man you know or are likely to know, as I promised to be in London within five days. The second reason that makes me seem pushy is that, given the chance, your antipodean friend would whisk you away to go fishing on a cold and rough lake on the other side of the world, and you will disappear for ever."

"Drown?" She relaxed. "I can swim quite well and I never go fishing."

"Worse than that. Disappear into obscurity and never fulfil your dreams."

"Dreams that only you can make come true?" Her incredulity made her voice sharp. "Are you really as arrogant as you sound?"

"Not arrogant, just frightened that I might lose the only woman I want to marry. Tomorrow when you are looking at American quilts and wondering how the women in covered-wagon days survived without a decent hairdresser, remember that I love you. What's for pudding?" he added with a very English inflexion, and turned the conversation to describing a set of exquisite shoes he had discovered in the museum, made of silk and costly embroidery and protected by wooden pattens when the wearer walked over mud.

"Better?" he asked as he saw her tension slacken.

"Better," she agreed and examined the small sketches he had done of some shrouded figures in the Abbey. "Are they for a project?"

"No, just a piece of self-indulgence. I like saints, and I would like to design sets and costumes for a medieval mystery play, possibly in Chartres or York."

"My ideas are far more mundane. I clothe the fairly affluent modern society and it pays the bills."

"You are taking time off now. When do you work again?"

"Soon. My manager will be restless if we don't begin a new collection and I have sent her a few ideas to work on. That takes us up to next spring and summer. We have sold the autumn and winter collections and a few one-off items for weddings and special awards dinners for actors and film people."

"You will be free by Christmas?"

"Yes. I give the workforce a few days off and we shut up shop until the New Year." Christmas? The thought of Christmas, the first away from Islington, Vincent and the others, had not occurred to her until Helmut spoke. "I have a standing invitation to visit my family in Canada, so I might go there this year," she said slowly, as if the idea was completely new and not very exciting.

"I don't envy you."

"You haven't met my family. They are quite normal and I happen to like them."

"I envy that part. I mean the cold. I do not envy that! Canada will be frozen solid, while I shall be swimming in a sea as warm as milk and soaking up the sun. Shall I send you a card smelling of suncream, saying 'Wish you were here'?"

"That's rotten! I could visit Vincent if he's got to California, and if I know Vincent he will try to be somewhere warm. He likes comfort."

"Or you could come to Australia with me. I'd share my sunscreen with you."

Her lips curved into a mocking smile. "Not New Zealand?"

"Too crowded unless Jake stays here for a long time. Besides he'd want you to watch him shear sheep or do something equally rewarding."

She ignored the jibe. "Turkey and plum pudding in that heat? Church in hot clothes?"

"Seafood and champagne and salad and maybe an outdoor service on the beach. They do have them if you feel the need to be religious."

"You see, you know so little about me. I may be very devout and belong to some weird cult or be an atheist. How about a Buddhist?"

"I can't imagine you in a veil, Muslim or nun, and I don't know if you could play the tambourine or sing spirituals with the clappy-happies. I don't think that is important. That is your business, but I can't think that you are Joan of Arc." He laughed, looking up at the ceiling. His throat was smooth and young and she wanted to kiss the firm laughing mouth.

"My stepmother tried to pair me off with a woman who went to such meetings."

"Was she pretty?"

"Solid and a good cook," he replied soberly. "She'll make someone a good *hausfrau* but her eyes had no sparkle as yours do and her breasts were not high and beautiful."

"Don't say such things," Penny retorted weakly.

"It is true. She had none of these things," he said with an innocent expression. "You will disappoint my stepmother as she wants me to marry a German and forget my English blood."

"I thought she eyed me with great approval. I felt threatened and had to escape from the museum before she tried to adopt me. I think I'll refrain from making dirndl skirts for my next summer collection and must throw away my recording of *The Sound of Music*, or I might be in real danger." She leaned over and tried to appear solemn. "Tell me, do you ever wear those leather knickers and snappy braces?"

"I have done so and drunk beer from vast steins, but I grew out of that." The electricity was palpable as they goaded each other with mild insults, fencing with words, watching and wanting and wishing that the table between them would vanish.

This should end in frantic kissing or more, Penny realised, and pushed back her chair. "Coffee in the lounge?" she said, thrusting back her hair as if shaking off a silken tether.

"If that's all that you offer."

"With sugar crystals."

"And mint chocolates. How did you know my weakness?"

"What weakness? I think you are a dangerous man who needs a woman like Frau Braun to keep you in order."

He looked complacent. "I am like my dog. I respond to

kind words and lots of love but I dig my feet in if I am dragged by the neck. Have you ever tried to drag a ton of unwilling dog if he wants to go the other way?"

"I know the feeling."

Helmut pulled her down beside him on a small settee, ignoring her move towards a safe armchair. "We cannot talk if you are a mile away," he said.

"The light is shining in my eyes," she protested.

"That is easily settled." He asked the waiter who arrived with the tray of coffee pots and cups to move back the offending lamp. "And I would like more *petits fours*," he added, eyeing the spartan selection on the small dish.

He took a tiny marzipan orange dipped in chocolate and delicately nibbled it. "You'll get fat if you eat those," Penny warned him, but his flat stomach and firm pectorals denied it. She recalled Vincent and the incipient paunch that could take over if he continued to take so little exercise. He would have to work-out if he was accepted for roles that needed a charismatic slim figure.

"There are many beautiful blonde and pneumatic German women who adore fat men," Helmut said calmly.

"With moustaches and underarm hair?" she asked sweetly.

"At least I'd be comfortable and well fed. Can you see me in tweed plus-twos and a deer-stalker hat, shrivelled up with self-denial and living half my life in a London club, to escape a carping British wife who watches every morsel that passes my lips?" was his answer as he took a coffee truffle.

She giggled. "I do know what you mean. I have an aunt and uncle like that."

"We do not visit them, ever! Do they have to be invited to the wedding?"

"Idiot. What wedding?"

"First, to be formal, we should be engaged. Tomorrow, if

you can forgo your tour of the American Museum, we can choose a ring."

"Tomorrow I am meeting Jake and spending the rest of the day with him."

"Tomorrow . . ." he began and turned her hand to kiss the palm.

"Cool it, Helmut," she said quietly. "I admit that I really do like you a lot, but I feel as if I weigh a ton and have four large feet firmly on the floor, pulling away from you." Her lips twitched. "Just call me Fido."

He put back a second truffle and sounded injured. "His name is Bruno." He smiled. "You are not even Brünnhilde; more Titania, the queen of the fairies, smelling of wild thyme and pease-blossom and driving me mad."

"Don't."

"Why not? Titania tried to have her forest and her secret spaces to herself and yet she had at last to go to her love."

"Having made a fool of herself," Penny said. "Thank you for reminding me. I have no desire to follow her by taking an ass for a lover."

"I wouldn't say that Jake is an ass," he replied in a reasonable tone. "Just not for you."

"You are impossible. Take me home, and leave me to sort out my clothes for tomorrow," she suggested.

"The day after tomorrow? Glastonbury Tor and Wells Cathedral?" She sensed what it cost his pride to beg but the anxiety was there.

"Ten o'clock at the coach station."

"Nine thirty at your door. I shall hire a car."

"Fine." She turned to face him as soon as they reached the door of the apartment. "Good-night . . . Helmut. It's been a wonderful evening."

"Tonight I am all British and you find it difficult to call me Helmut. A silly name that makes English people think I am a piece of armour. My stepmother insists on using it, but I have an English name that my mother gave me. A name is important. I like yours as it means faithful love, as Odysseus found with his Penelope, but I think you could never marry a man called Helmut."

She laughed softly. "That's a very shrewd remark and true. It could be one reason for going back to London soon and alone."

He pulled a small velvet envelope from his pocket. "I know you are not ready for a ring, but wear this if you will."

"A St Christopher medallion?" She turned the small gold disc over and it felt warm in her hand. "Christopher?" He nodded. "Your name is Christopher?"

"Yes, my British friends prefer it."

"I do, too. Hello, Chris."

He kissed her slowly but with a passion that was more intense for his restraint, then walked away and left her to turn the key in the door.

Seven

Penny closed the transom window in the kitchen and mopped the water from the windowsill. Rain beat on the glass, and the street outside the apartment was gleaming grey with wet. Taxis with lights on their roofs and the rear lights of other cars pushing the muddy spray into the gutters were the only moving things to show any colour.

It was odd to be dressing in a raincoat and soft leather boots, but as well as being a wet morning, the air was chilly. Garden party weather, her aunt would say and wondered each year why so many events took place when it was usual for a calamitous change in the weather to put the sun to flight and send expensively dressed guests running from the thunder and lightning into the draughty marquees.

Clearing later, the radio weatherman had said without much conviction, and a visit to the Abbey seemed a better choice than a wait by a bus stop in the rain and a walk up the long drive to the American Museum.

She picked up a large sling bag and added a plastic bag and some shoes. If the rain cleared, boots would feel heavy and look incongruous in the sun so she would need to change into something lighter. At least her straw hat wouldn't have an airing and Jake couldn't tease her about it. She found a rain-repellent silk scarf that should protect her hair, opened her folding umbrella and ventured out into the street.

Jake, she thought. Today I am with Jake. Everything was

different: a different companion, and even Bath looked like any other city with grey stones and dark skies, the warmth gone from the thick walls and the air feeling heavy with the moisture that in winter made Bath a bad place for sufferers with chest complaints who had to live there.

She knew she had to tear her mind away from Helmut . . . Chris. He really did have a dual personality that intrigued her, but today it would be Jake, the more easy-going and boyish uncomplicated Jake, and she looked forward to an amusing day . . . weather permitting.

He waved from the bus shelter by the stop for the coach and she splashed across the road just in time to board the vehicle.

"Thought you'd forgotten," Jake said in greeting.

Water dripped from the now folded umbrella. "Wouldn't have missed it for anything," she lied, conscious of a trickle of rain down her neck.

"Sure, what's a drop of rain? They'd be grateful for this back home just now. We need it to make the grass grow in time for the first spring bite and the hay. It was a shock to see the back-to-front seasons here, and the water in the bath going down the hole the wrong way."

"Yours is the wrong way, not ours," she corrected him.

He went on talking about crops and wiped a circle of mist from the window, eyeing with approval the wall of water slanting into the road.

"Almost enough to go rafting," Penny said. "I'd rather have the sun."

"Cold?" He clasped her hand in a brotherly way and she sat close to him. "It's great to see you again," he said, his hand clasp becoming less brotherly, his smile more serious. He leaned over and sniffed her hair. "Christ! Damp hair is a real turn on."

She withdrew her hand and stiffened. "Down, boy, it's not

time for snacks." This was no shaggy sheepdog to be coaxed. He was a far more eager rampant male springer spaniel who needed fending off, not dragging along behind her.

The coach driver took his passengers right to the door of the museum and Penny was only too willing to give the expected tip. Inside the Ladies, she changed from her boots and dried her hair, lamenting that the so-called rainproof scarf, wasn't. Maybe Gertrude could find a solution to the problem that came each wet day for women who hated wearing hats, and when umbrellas were liable to blow inside out in high winds. Her interest quickened. It had been tried by many manufacturers but none had been completely successful; at best they provided some protection and at worst they looked and crackled like plastic bags storing lettuces. They must talk about that. A siliconed raincoat and matching scarf that didn't smell of wax and yet was efficient, light and attractive, would sell very well and become an essential item in every handbag.

Jake was lounging against a fine oak tallboy, oblivious to the fact that his wet anorak was making damp marks on the polished wood. "Not making notes already? We haven't seen anything yet."

"Just an idea for a decent rainscarf," she replied sweetly and laughed at his expression. "Neither of us can get away from what we do in the real world," she insisted. "You assessed the rain for crops and I thought of an idea for my salon and workshops."

"Clothes? You call that important? Come on, I smell gingerbread."

He went into the huge kitchens and accepted a large gingerbread man from a smiling woman dressed in a gingham gown and white muslin cap, leaving Penny to examine the bookstall and the many illustrated pamphlets and books for sale. She was soon engrossed and it was half an hour later when Jake came looking for her that she surfaced from American history and dress and folklore.

"They have tools and farming equipment that must have come from the Ark," he said. "I saw the same kind of thing in the museum in Dunedin in South Island so I suppose all pioneer people had similar things." He hovered at her side, impatiently. "They're starting a video of cattle-ranching as it was and as it is now in the States where they have miles of land, just as we have."

She smiled. "I'll be here when you are finished," she promised. "No, I don't want to see it. Really!"

She admired the wonderful bed quilts that had been made with such care, perhaps to be handed down as family heirlooms, and she bought a few pieces of needlework for friends.

Was that what life had been like for the pioneer women? Was the success of a quilt the highlight of their lives? She shivered. What if a woman had ambition and original ideas that had nothing to do with farming? Were they allowed any other life than sewing, cooking and child-bearing? Fine if that's what they wanted, but what if they had visions of more?

"I'm hungry." Jake put his packet of boiled sweets into his pocket and asked Penny if she could stow some ginger biscuits in her sling bag. "Come on, real food," he said and led her to the café. "You know, this reminds me of home. My mother sews a lot and my sister bakes good cake."

"Great." Penny smiled but it was an effort. Here was this good-looking guy with more than a fair share of testosterone, ready to take her if she allowed it to happen, and yet she felt stifled when he talked of his background. I could love you, as far as good sex is concerned, she thought, but I couldn't live like that.

She ate the meat in her steak and kidney pie and left the

rather solid pastry, while Jake ate every scrap put before him and talked about New Zealand and the future, as if it was a fact that she would go there with him and be there for ever. "You'll love it," he repeated for the fifth time.

"What did you see at the theatre before you came away?" she asked, when she could stop the flow and get a word in.

He stopped eating for a puzzled moment. "You mean plays?"

"Yes."

"Can't say. We do have television," he offered. "You'd feel at home as they show mostly British and American soaps."

"You do have theatres? Concerts?"

"Sure we do, in Auckland and Christchurch I suppose. We went to Shakespeare at school but I haven't been since. College had a group of players but they did heavy stuff and nobody bothered, or not in my circle." His eyes brightened. "You should have seen our sports complex. It was out of this world and I even did a bit of fencing."

"Book shops?" she asked hopefully.

"Lots of racks of paperbacks like they have at airports and some book shops in the big towns. You'll feel really at home. They have all the British and American bestsellers. There's a good library in Rotorua, my mother says," he added, when he saw that she was unimpressed.

"I take it you don't read a lot?"

He smiled indulgently. "Never get bored enough for that."

"I know. Don't say it again, Jake. I'll love it, or you think I would do if I went there, but I'm not going to New Zealand in the near or distant future." She got up. "The rain has stopped. Let's see the gardens. I've had enough of the homely country kitchen life."

"I thought you'd enjoy looking at the craft work."

"Not when it tells me of women sitting for hours sewing tiny stitches by hand in dim lamplight, making work that would be too good to use so it was put away in bottom drawers for the next generation of housebound women to keep as status symbols."

"That's what women *do*! Don't you want a home and family?"

"No, I like my work and my independence."

They were in a small area of grass and burgeoning rose bushes, not quite in bloom. He seized her by the shoulders and kissed her with hard angry lips. "Don't say that. You were made for love and children and . . . everything. I dream of you all night and I think of you all day. I think that just to know I could come home to you would be a wonderful feeling; to see you every day and to sit together, make love and eat together."

"Every day?"

"Of course."

"You wouldn't be there every day," she pointed out. "The men get together to go hunting and fishing and drinking, or so you told me, and you said I could set up my own business if I wanted it, so that would take me away, too."

"You'd do that from home. Have a sewing room built on specially," he offered.

"Personally, I don't sit and sew. My work isn't like that. I have to have a studio and a lot of people making up the designs."

A large raindrop eased along the bent branch of an overhanging shrub and fell on his hair, making a strand fall darkly across his sun-touched brow. You are beautiful, she thought, and her viscera cramped up but it wasn't because of her period. His hair was thick and shining and he had cut himself shaving too quickly that morning, making her want to rub away the bead of dried blood and kiss it better.

His voice was husky. "When you look at me like that I want to take you under that tree and make love to you."

"Too wet and uncomfortable. I'd get pneumonia and creepy-crawlies." Her voice was shaky and she tried to get away. "You are hurting me and I can't breathe." She knew that she was almost as aroused as Jake and her breath was ragged, not just because he was holding her too closely.

He released her but looked triumphant. "You are one cool lady but not as immune to me as you think." His expression changed to one of comic dismay. "You'll have to say yes and quickly. I can't stay for more than a few days and I want you with me. What happened to time? Penny, I know we've not been together for long enough for most people to be sure, but I am very sure. Let's not fool around. I know what I want. I want to marry you and take you home."

"This is my home," she said quietly. "I love my work and I can't uproot in five minutes to leave it all and make a home among strangers."

He made a rude dismissive gesture. "I've never felt like this about anyone, and I know you want me too. I see no problem. They'll love you at home."

"And I'll love them and your life there?"

"Sure! You can go back to London to pack and I'll book a flight with me next week. We'll be back in time for the big rodeo."

She tried to be patient and objective. "Tickets and visas and money take time, and what do I say to my employees? Sorry but you're out of a job. Bad luck but you'll manage. Just leave the work you started. It can gather dust until I send for it?" She giggled. "My accountant would go spare, and my manager would kill me. I am the creative element and my ideas sell the clothes. It isn't a case of someone taking over a computer!"

"You can do it. I know it can't be easy," he conceded. "You have plenty of people who could take over and run the business if it's firmly established. I admit that I didn't know that so many people were involved, but this is *us*, and we must take what we want."

"You haven't listened. I said that my ideas *are* the firm and without me the whole set-up would crumble. It is very important to a lot of people, not just me." She was exasperated. "You take too much for granted. Have you ever been refused anything, Jake?"

"Not a lot." He seemed very sure of himself and complacent.

"No girlfriend has given you the elbow?"

He blushed. "Not really. She wasn't important and it wasn't for real. We didn't play the same games and she went on to be a tennis champion, so we drifted apart."

"She didn't want to settle down on the farm?" Her raised eyebrows conveyed her sarcasm. "Well, well, I'm not alone."

"I was never in love with her. She lived on the next unit and her family thought I'd bring her into line when she wanted out. She'd always been difficult."

"Full marks to her," Penny said quietly. "A girl with a mind of her own."

"She wanted me."

"No need to be defensive. I'm sure she did. You are easy to want."

"She slept with me!"

"And got that bit over so that she could concentrate on her life away from you?" She sounded gentle and a little sad. "Maybe I should do that, but I doubt if you would be satisfied, and I would feel deprived if I really loved you and we drifted apart. Just now, I am the angel at the top of the Christmas tree, a thing to be desired and reached for, but what if you found the tinsel dress fragile and the doll bruised with over-familiar treatment and having to be pushed aside for more important matters?"

"It couldn't be like that."

"Don't sulk. You know it could happen. The honeymoon would be wonderful and something to remember all our lives, but what after that?"

"It would last for ever."

"I lived with Vincent but refused to marry him. After a while he stopped asking me, until he thought he might lose me. So then he tried to make it legal and have me for life. I know how close I came to living an existence that would have been boring and cloistered and I doubt if I want to be married to anyone. I know I escaped a life that even if it suited Vincent, working in the so-called glamour of films, for me it would have lacked the thrill that he found and would have been full of the mundane background to his life, while my own creativity filtered away. He complained often enough that I spent too much time on my own work and paid little heed to his interests."

"You couldn't have been in love."

"You mean that if I truly loved someone I would do as he wanted and submerge my own career?"

"I guess so, but with me, you wouldn't be losing out, you'd gain so much."

She smiled sadly. First Chris and now Jake had the conviction that she would be happy with him alone. "You must have been in love with other women?"

"Not like this. The first time I saw you I was hit for six."

"When do you leave for home?"

"Alone?" It seemed to be getting through that she might possibly refuse him.

"Alone. I do love you, Jake, but I know it's only a physical feeling. We'd have nothing in common on a day-to-day basis."

He held her close and his agony made her want to weep. "Think about it and come out to New Zealand later. You might change your mind. Promise?"

"I'll think about a holiday there."

"Meanwhile, could you, could we, just once?"

"Make love?"

"It might make all the difference. You might find me irresistible," he said with an attempt at a wicked laugh.

"To be frank, as I feel now, I'd like that, but it's physically impossible."

He looked absurdly like a baby who has been deprived of a goody. "Hell, Penny, I thought every woman was on the Pill."

"Thanks for your romantic understanding. Let's get back before it rains again. I feel the need for a visit to the Abbey coming on."

"Can't we go back to your place and talk?"

She smiled. "That would be too frustrating for you."

"Not entirely." He kissed her and his hands found her breasts through the thin shirt. "I could be satisfied with heavy petting."

"I think the air of sanctity would be good for us," she replied. "And there are people coming into the garden, so we'd better go."

"Are you angry?"

"Not really, but you are a bit overpowering. I could go off you when you talk like that."

The drift of the hills on which Bath was built, seven like Rome, some said, lay green and terracotta where houses had appeared among trees and gardens, and the afternoon sunlight played gently on drying roof-tops and the grey stone of the city below the museum as the storm passed into the Mendips and along the river.

In the bus, Jake examined several leaflets that he had taken from the information kiosk at the museum. He had regained his laid-back attitude and his humour. "What now? I can't take the Roman Baths again and we've seen the museum. It's too late for Cheddar, you don't like rafting and I'll not be hungry for at least another hour."

Penny relented. "OK, no Abbey. Let's just walk about and see Bath. I do it each morning and can't see enough of it. We can stop in the Abbey square and you can buy me an ice-cream and watch the jugglers and buskers." She said it in fun as if giving a child a treat and was quite shocked to find that he was enthusiastic.

"Great idea. I saw a guy with psychedelic juggling clubs that flashed and seemed to move very fast, and he was good. I think I'll try it when I get home. We can have competitions."

As they sat on a bench by the group of students who had re-emerged to continue their entertainment now that the rain had stopped and visitors were venturing out again, she felt a surge of tenderness for him. She reached up and kissed his cheek. "You are a sweet boy and I like you a lot, but what would we do on rainy days?"

"Make love."

She shook her head. "I would need to work and plan and to speak to friends in my own trade, and even to read and talk about books and music and the theatre. I like concerts and I go to all the plays at the Old Vic and the National in London."

"There would be other things to take their place," he said eagerly. "You wanted to see Maori crafts. They are great and you can't see them unless you come back with me."

"If I can, I'll take a holiday there and let you know when

I'm leaving England. More than that I can not promise. Go back soon or you'll miss the rodeo."

"I might as well," he said sullenly. "I do have an air ticket for Friday. I was going to cancel it."

"I shall miss you."

"Then come with me."

"Later, if I can. Now I have to telephone my manager and give her some idea of when I shall be back in London. I do work hard for my living." She regarded the students with amusement. "Stay here, Jake. It's going to be good. I'll pop into the Abbey for five minutes and then go back. See you later, maybe."

"Give me your phone number?"

"My London one will find out where I am at any time, if you really need to be in touch, but you have a lot going for you at home, and with all those sheep you'll have far too much to do rather than mooning over a woman you met for a few days on holiday."

"Take my address. You must come out there. We have to meet again." He looked blankly at the business card she gave him. "Christ! You really are saying goodbye!"

"I hope we do meet again," she said and smiled. "Not goodbye, Jake." She kissed him and he held her tightly and when she broke away and walked towards the Abbey, they both had tears in their eyes.

Eight

The huge doors of the Abbey were open and a trickle of tourists moved slowly into the dim space beyond. Instinctively, Penny opened her bag to find a scarf to cover her head and found only the repellent cold damp one she had worn earlier. Americans and Germans in T-shirts, shorts and hatless, and some women in halter tops and skimpy boob tubes, ignored notices asking for restraint in dress and she shrugged away her reservations. At least she was neat, her legs and arms were modestly covered, and the Anglicans were more tolerant of unsuitable dress than were the Catholics and the Greeks.

The familiar smell of old churches pervaded the atmosphere with the fading scent of the last incense burned that day at the early service. The benison of cool stones and ancient memories made her slow down and want to keep out the heat and hassle of the Abbey precincts. She gazed up at the soaring roof space and the delicate tracery of the rood screen and wandered down the aisle to a side chapel where two people knelt in prayer, a reminder that this was primarily a house of worship. She slipped into the seat behind them and bent her head.

A prayer for Jake might be in order, she thought, now that she knew that she might never see him again. He really was suffering – for the moment, at least. She knew that a clean break would help him to get over his infatuation more easily.

I've known him for such a short time, she told herself, it can't mean that much to him. But an uneasy feeling told her that he had sailed through life so far, having most things coming easily, and she had been a shock to his pride, holding out against his charm and saying quite firmly that they had no lasting future together. He might be convinced, as he had said many times, that she was the love of his life.

The choir was being taken through an anthem by a tall man in an academic gown with a stern and set expression, who looked as if he was drilling a battalion of army recruits and not a bunch of men and boys singing to the glory of God. The choir was not dressed for a service, only for rehearsal in jeans and shirts and jackets, which made it seem unreal. Later, in cassocks and fresh frilled collars, they would assume the dignity and beauty of the Abbey, the voluminous garments hiding their physical deficiences, but now they looked so ordinary.

Penny went over to the rack of small candles. Why do I feel the urge to light candles in strange churches? she wondered. She did it in Greece and France and Spain and found a kind of peace in the act, often remembering friends who had died long ago, like the child at school who had died of leukaemia. I had forgotten her, and my cousin Andrew who died of polio in India, but here, I suddenly think of them. One sandy tray was empty and she hoped that the custodian had left the burning candles long enough for the prayer to reach heaven before they were rudely extinguished. The smell of spent wax faded and she paused undecided, then felt in her bag for some money.

She opened her purse, knowing that each candle needed a few coins to contribute to the Abbey's funds, but there were only bank notes that were too much and small coins which were less than she wanted to give.

"Allow me. How many candles do you want?"

"Chris?" Her pleasure was evident.

"I'm glad you use that name," he said. "It's good to see you." He paused and the silence grew warm, his smile friendly and intimate, but the touch on her arm was no threat.

"What are you doing here? I thought you had been to the Abbey several times."

"I like it, and I knew that at some time I would find you here. Today I was right. I saw Jake trying to juggle with the buskers – they seem to be giving him lessons. There was another Kiwi there and he seemed quite happy to be with him. I thought you might have slipped away to somewhere more peaceful, so I came here and found an angel lighting candles for the souls of the wicked."

She watched him take a candle and light it from another in the tray. "Do you do this often?"

It sounded trite, like the old phrase when a new dancing partner has no conversation.

"Sometimes, in foreign churches, but at home my father is very low church and I hardly ever enter a church of any kind. My mother was nominally Church of England."

"I want to light three candles." She watched him put far more coins than was necessary into the box and smiled her thanks. "It is different here," she agreed. "I went to a convent school and the smell of incense is a good memory, but I never did accept their communion though the nuns were really kind and I had a good education."

He watched her light her candles and added one more of his own. "Am I allowed to know for whom you pray?" he said.

"Two friends who died."

"And the third one?"

"For me, I suppose. I'm confused since I came here, just

when I expected a fairly simple and even boring few weeks to let me feel my own space. I need some guidance."

"I lit one for my mother and one now for us."

"Doesn't that seem like sacrilege?" She felt stifled.

"Nothing sacrilegious about my feelings for you, Penny, but it must not worry you. I have learned to cut my losses and we can be friends if that satisfies you." He laughed softly when he saw that she was still disturbed. "I can only do my best, and this is one way to hedge my bets. I have a feeling I need all the help I can get, from whatever benign source it comes."

Penny's tension released into soft laughter. "You pray to whatever gods are handy? I thought I was the only one who did that. I light candles wherever I find an old church in whatever country I happen to be and when I was on a cruiser in the Aegean, I tipped wine overboard as a libation to Athena to give us soft winds, and to Poseidon for peaceful anchorages."

"Did it work?"

"Mostly, apart from one bad storm."

"Was Vincent there?"

She eyed him sharply and saw the careful nonchalance that concealed his real thoughts. "Yes, we were with a party of theatre people and one rising star who's now famous. In fact, she's in the same soap that Vincent is with now. Maybe they will get together. I know she fancied him at the time, but I heard that she married one of the sponsors of 'The Smiling Lake Saga'."

"Were you all good sailors?"

"All but Vincent and one other male actor. They groaned a lot."

"I am a good sailor."

"I'm sure!" Her scathing glance was to put him down a little. "Vincent has other abilities in his favour." It was a mild reproach to warn him not to tot up the pluses and minuses that he could put against Vincent's score as a possible rival.

"Have you finished here? I've been sketching a knight on a tomb and think he was a Templar."

"Crossed feet and a familiar at his feet? Chainmail and hauberk with the cross? I saw him and wondered how long it took a craftsman to make each link of that vest."

"So back to metal shirts in the next collection?"

"My team would mutiny, and it would never get off the catwalk. Who would wear it in the high street other than a ghost rattling its chains?"

They walked out into the sunshine and Penny put on dark glasses. She glanced towards the buskers but Jake had gone. A sense of loss made her glad that Chris couldn't read her eyes, and for a moment she felt that she had been too hard on him and wanted Jake to appear, smiling and confident as he'd been at the American Museum.

"Cup of tea?" asked Chris, and her mind slipped away from Jake.

"Only if it's in the Pump Rooms." Jake would have gone to the café on the bridge if he wanted refreshment now, she thought wryly. The scones were better there and much bigger and he didn't feel comfortable in the sedate and upmarket atmosphere of the Regency rooms.

"Wise choice," Chris said and she knew that he had similar thoughts. Belatedly, he asked if she had plans for the rest of the day that included Jake.

"No, I think he's busy. He returns to New Zealand on Friday. I said goodbye to him today, but I expect I shall bump into him if I'm not careful. I hate goodbyes."

"And what are your plans?"

"A day or so here and then back to work," she said firmly.

"I'm restless now and need to be back in London, but we are going to Glastonbury tomorrow?"

"A full day I hope, as I have rented a car and we can take our time."

"It sounds bliss after running for wet, smelly buses like I did today."

"I shall take a camera and a sketch pad. And you?"

"I had the same idea. Usually I forget and wish that I had recorded places in more detail."

He was so easy to be with. They sat at a small table and ordered toasted Bath buns and Earl Grey tea and the small tea-time orchestra played gems from almost-forgotten musicals and simple classics. Groups of Japanese listened politely but without much comprehension to the alien tunes, as they lined up to sample the spa water and obediently drank it without flinching. They took rolls of film of each other, the spa water fountain and the orchestra.

"Penny?"

"Yes? You seem embarrassed. Don't tell me you've found someone you'd prefer to spend the day with?" She mocked him gently.

"No, I want to have you to myself for a whole day more than anything. I have the car now and asked Lars and Gertrude to be my guests this evening, not at the hotel but to drive and find a good pub for a simple meal. There are four seats in the car and only three to fill them. If you have made no arrangements with Jake, would you join us?"

"Brilliant! I want to talk to Gertrude again before they leave and I had thought of getting in touch today now that I'm not seeing Jake again."

"Never again?"

"I'm not sure. He has my London address but I shan't see him again in Bath unless we happen to meet or he arrives uninvited at the apartment. If I pass by New Zealand I might drop in to visit him. I like him a lot and hope we can be friends."

Chris let out his breath slowly as if he'd run a race, but he sounded almost formal. "Thank you for accepting. That will be a pleasure for us all."

Penny was surprised to see that the Pump Room staff were clearing tables in a way that said the place was closing for the afternoon. "I must go back and change before this evening. Smart, or flat shoes and jeans?"

"Be comfortable, but I can't imagine Gertrude in sandals or sweatshirts, can you? I'll be very good and not make you all walk down muddy lanes."

"Do I meet the others or wait for you?"

"I'll collect them first and call for you at seven."

As she opened the door, the phone rang. "Penny? I've been trying to get you. Why don't you have an answering machine?" grumbled Josie.

"I'm on holiday and I'm having a peaceful time, or I was until now. What's the trouble?"

"Sorry to butt in, and it's probably nothing, but there seems to be some mail from America waiting in the studio and we all know that Vincent wouldn't put pen to paper unless he wanted something rather badly."

"He could phone you."

"Not Vincent. He knows what I think of him and he wouldn't trust me to send on phone messages. I once told him that my phone was business only and if he wanted you he must use your line and leave messages on your answer phone, so if he does ring it will be on your private answer phone and I'm not touching that. All the business calls come to me in the office and that's quite enough to handle."

"You and he never did get on, but he's not that bad!" Penny chuckled. "He does know that you never joined the

Vincent Admiration Society. He's half afraid of you, but surely if it was anything urgent he wouldn't hesitate to use you."

"Do you want the mail sent on?"

"No, I shall be back by the weekend or just after that, and I have no intention of letting Vincent ruin my holiday by telling me some whinge he thinks I ought to know about."

"You *have* changed."

"That is very true. I've had time to distance myself and I feel free of him for the first time."

"Who is he?"

"What?"

"It takes another guy to rub out the first one," Josie said airily. "Don't I know it?"

"What makes you think it's only one?"

"Get away! There can't be more than one sexy man in Bath. I've been there. It rained!"

"They aren't all philistines like you."

"So I don't send on anything? Not even the holiday brochures? By the way, I love the sketches. There is one thing you might or might not like to know."

"Don't tell me now. I have a date for this evening and one tomorrow and I want to enjoy the last of the time here. No need to send anything. I'll deal with Vincent when I get back and not until then, and we'll arrange to meet to discuss what I suggested."

"I'll be glad to have you back and hear what you think of my ideas too . . . and we must talk seriously about expanding." Josie put down the phone and thought it was unnecessary to add that one large envelope had come from an airline and she suspected that it might be details of a flight to America.

Penny tried to forget that Josie had rung and yet she knew that Vincent was either in trouble or trying to blackmail her into joining him because he missed her. She tightened her mouth. He missed her because she was no longer there to back him up, look decorative and make him feel good.

"Are you feeling well? You seem worried," Lars said as soon as she appeared at the front door and saw Chris and Lars standing there.

"Not really worried. My manager rang and suddenly all sorts of problems have arisen that might take me back early."

"Forget them for tonight," Chris said, but he seemed concerned for her. "By the way, we saw your Kiwi friend and he was looking for you. Do you want to see him, Penny?"

"No. I said goodbye and it would be pointless to meet again here."

Chris smiled and she knew that he was feeling good. "It's going to be a fine evening and I heard of a very pleasant pub near Limpley Stoke. Do you know how we get there, Penny?"

"Yes, it's a lovely spot, not far from Bath, but promise that we don't have to walk along the canal. Gertrude isn't dressed for that and I'm not keen to be bitten by midges."

"After walking round Clifton in Bristol all afternoon, I would be incapable of anything other than a drink and food and a nice view."

"Gertrude was fascinated by the Clifton Suspension Bridge and we walked over it and back again and then over the Downs," Lars explained.

They slipped into what was now their normal warm and casual relationship and Penny forgot Vincent and Josie and the mountain of mixed mail that must be gathering at the studio.

Gertrude exclaimed with pleasure when she saw the sweep of the deep valley and the canal. "Yehudi Menuhin, who played often in Bath, was supposed to have thought that this view is one of the finest in England and his favourite," Penny said.

"If you are going home this week, we may have time to meet and discuss work? I would like to see your workplace before we go home," Gertrude said when they had been served steaks and salad and house red wine. She regarded Penny thoughtfully and asked quietly, with a glance at the two men who were engrossed in a discussion about the Swedish economy, "Why are you cutting down your holiday? Is it Jake?"

"Not really, but he does come into it. He thinks he is in love with me and it would be only a matter of time and much effort to make me decide to go with him to New Zealand. What he doesn't know is that each time we meet I see aspects of his life that would put me off for ever, even though I find him terribly sexy. He's too physical for me just now. If only he would cool it, he might have had more success. Men are so sure of their charms that they fail to see that a woman might not agree with everything they say."

"Like Vincent? I think you've heard from him."

"Not directly." She told Gertrude of the phone call and sounded resentful.

"He still holds a thread or two," Gertrude said. "Habits are hard to break."

"We are finished. I have at least learned that. Selling everything and refusing to go with him to America was more than just a hint! Two men being attracted to me has inflated my ego no end and given me confidence." She looked at Chris and saw that he was watching her and she blushed, but she thought he hadn't heard what she said.

"He is very nice," Gertrude said wickedly.

"You don't have to tell me that."

"And different?"

Penny laughed. "Jake was all for pulling me into bed to

convince me what a wonderful lover he'd be, but the other one hardly touches me," she said in a near whisper.

"Much more dangerous."

"What are you whispering about?" asked Lars.

"Men, of course," Gertrude replied calmly. "Why do you talk politics when I want some ice-cream?"

They sat by a picture window and watched the lights come on in Bath. The fading light made the canal a twisting line of anthracite edged by dark trees but the shadows were not sinister and a faint light came from a narrowboat anchored for the night by the bridge.

Penny wondered who was in the boat. Were they married with a family or lovers alone and discovering each other?

Chris, on his way back from ordering more coffee at the bar, leaned over her shoulder to see what she was watching. "Some day, I want to take a boat like that along the Canal du Midi in the south of France."

"Why there?" She felt the warmth of his body against her back and his hands lingered on her shoulders. He touched her hair, lifting a tendril gently, then stood back, away from all contact.

"It would be warm and romantic and exciting."

"You would also be devoured by mosquitoes," Lars said dryly.

"Do you get bitten?" Chris asked, as if it was important.

"Yes. They love me."

"We could burn a sulphur candle on deck and pull down the hatch and be safe," he said.

"Perhaps the people with you would be immune to bugs," Penny said lightly.

"I would have only one person on board, and I have great faith in the power of candles. I lit one today and you are here tonight."

"Now who is whispering?" Gertrude asked.

"Time to go before the midges get you." Chris laughed and asked for the bill. "At least on Glastonbury Tor the breeze will keep away all flying insects, and my candle will continue to bring me luck."

Gertrude eyed him with amusement. "I notice you haven't invited us tomorrow in that nice big car."

"You have seen Glastonbury and Wells and I think you would not be happy climbing hills." He kissed her cheek. "You are not invited," he said in a low voice. "I shall see you in London as soon as I get there, but if you tease me, I shall invite you to dinner with my stepmother."

"You are a very cruel man."

"Why should I suffer alone? Perhaps Penny will come with me to have dinner with Frau Braun."

"You will be in London next week? I had forgotten, but I aim to be busy that evening."

"What evening?"

"Whichever is the one it is you have in mind," she said sweetly.

"But you will meet me in London?"

"We'll talk about it tomorrow if we think we can stand each other after walking up the Tor."

Chris drove them back to Bath and Penny asked to be dropped off first. "You can take Gertrude and Lars back and park for the night. It would be silly to make a return journey."

"See you tomorrow at nine thirty," he said.

"See you in London," Lars said. "I shall visit the sex shows in Soho if Gertrude spends too long with you gloating over fashion."

Nine

"We'll go to Glastonbury first before we have lunch. After that we shall be less energetic, so we can wander round Wells Cathedral." Chris regarded Penny with approval. Her crimson moleskin trousers were smart and practical and the pale chambray cotton shirt, knotted below her breasts, was cool and pretty.

"We shall be dry today," she said.

"And safe," he added solemnly.

"How do you know that?"

"You are wearing the St Christopher medallion."

The slender chain was visible but the gold disc was nestling between her breasts. "It could be anything on this chain," she retorted, but pulled it free to show that it was as he said, the St Christopher, and she left it resting on the shirt, oddly pleased that she could show that she wore it.

A delicious sense of adventure now that they were alone made her eyes bright. Chris was fun and not pushy and yet there was this edge of awareness that flickered between them, enough to make the day exciting.

Green fields and blossom-filled gardens against grey walls made the drive pleasant and Penny began to wonder if she was as devoted to city life as she'd supposed. A cottage on the outskirts of a town like Bath might be very satisfying and give her the best of two worlds. She saw a long low stone building in the garden of a large house and knew it could make a wonderful spacious workplace, as it had been for hundreds of years, but with fabrics and fashion, not the wood and stone of the old carpenters and stonemasons who had used the bothy and may even have helped to build the Abbey.

Living with Vincent and working amidst the stimulus of a busy area had been her main interest for so long that the fresh look and smell of the country was almost a shock. She was amazed that so little of England was as the pessimists said, covered with concrete. Even the much hated motorways were becoming softened by the green verges and banks of wild flowers and rogue bushes. She saw a hawk hovering over what was for him now safe territory and a good hunting ground for voles and rabbits, as few people apart from workmen and farmers could walk on the banks or invade the neighbouring rough ground.

"You are quiet," Chris said.

"So are you. I'm enjoying being driven and watching the fields." She laughed. "Not many fields and much more traffic in Islington."

"It's good to have a companion who doesn't chatter all the time and doesn't tell me how to drive."

"Frau Braun?"

"Sometimes I feel like stopping and telling her to drive," he said grimly. "It is better when we are on a coach. She can then revile the driver and I can go to sleep."

"Does she drive well?"

"She doesn't drive. Non-drivers are the worst as they see no problems and think it's as easy as driving a toy scooter."

A hedge heavy with pink and white dog roses flashed by and a garden scarlet with old-fashioned red hot pokers made Penny remember the garden in Devon with nostalgia. "I ought to go to Devon again soon," she said.

"Not today! I don't feel like driving that far in this car."
He grinned. "Any other time I shall love it. Where shall we
stay and when do you want to leave?"

"Idiot," she said softly. "It was just a sudden thought
when I saw those flowers back there."

"What are they called?"

"I've no idea of the Latin name, but we called them
red hot pokers and they grew almost wild in our garden."
She sank lower in her seat and frowned. "It was just
an association of ideas. I have no real roots there now
apart from memories of a very happy childhood. They've
all gone, my family and neighbours, and in one way it
might be a mistake to go back and find it all changed.
I haven't returned since my parents went to Canada three
years ago, and even then there were changes that began
to make the village look like any other, with banks and
building societies and take-aways. Who knows, the people
who own the house may not like red hot pokers and have
grubbed them up to make the kind of formal flowerbeds
that my mother loathes? The garden may be a deluge of
regimented begonias now."

"You never took Vincent there?" He sounded casual but
waited for her reply.

"No." She bit her lip. "He suggested it once but I put
it off. I knew he'd hate it; the small town where nobody
would be impressed by him apart from him being my
boyfriend. My family were well known but he would
have been unimportant to the locals. They wouldn't have
liked his taste in ties and the fact that in their opinion he wasn't suitable for the daughter of their local ex-
mayor."

"Is that true?" He sounded mock alarmed. "Perhaps I
should withdraw my offer to take you there, but I do have
nice ties."

"They'd like you," Penny said and blushed.

"Thank you. That's the nicest thing you've said to me so don't spoil it by saying you didn't mean it."

"It's true. Some people would not be welcome there and some would. That's all," she said, trying to sound practical. "Vincent tries to impress people wherever he goes and the average Devonian innkeeper wouldn't want to know. He'd be polite, call him me dear or lover, and dismiss him as an upstart."

"Each time you mention Vincent, I think you discover something more about him, most of it bad. I can't think that you ever really loved him." Chris stared ahead and his face gave nothing away but she sensed that he enjoyed hearing of Vincent's less than perfect character.

"I'm just sounding like a bitch. I do love him in many ways, but being away from him lets me take an objective view and I remember all the things that I didn't like, but made myself ignore. He's a very nice kind man and I learned a lot from him."

"Relax. Don't sound so defensive. I'm sure he is a paragon under that odd picture you paint of him."

She sighed. "Sometimes we can't see people properly, however well we know them, until we are at a distance and then they disappoint us."

"Only the ones who have no lasting place in our lives. Whenever I see you, I see you afresh, my heart leaps and I love what I see."

"You don't know me at all," she replied stubbornly, but recalled her own wonder that morning when he came to collect her for the day, his face wreathed in smiles of anticipation like a child ready for a special treat.

" 'He had forgotten that she was so fair and that her neck curved down in such a way.' "

"I am not Helen of Troy!"

"No? The poet was right, rediscovering you each day would be miraculous."

"Stop it, Chris. I can't listen to what you say as I know it's unreal."

"So long as you know how I feel," he replied and his expression told her that he knew just how she was reacting, too.

Glastonbury was recovering from a "Happening" and the road was full of decrepit cars and wagons coming away from the town as hippies left for other festivals.

"Flower power seems to flourish here," Chris said. "I suppose it has another name now, but 'travellers' doesn't have the same nostalgic ring."

"You sound wistful. Does it appeal to you?" She glanced at the well-cut shirt and trousers and his immaculate finger-nails and couldn't imagine him in a caftan or grubby clothes. If he grew his hair long it would fall in waves and be clean and soft, she decided. That might be good, but not a pony-tail.

"I tried the Katmandu trail when I was seventeen, found that I hated it and hitched back to civilisation," he admitted. "It was the done thing and I had to keep quiet about the fact that I found it boring and sordid, as my friends laughed at anyone not going away and trying life and sex and drugs."

"But you like travelling; that's what you said."

"I like travelling but that trip decided me that I wanted to earn enough to do it properly and see the real wonders of the world. Imagine spending weeks in India without seeing anything but the dust and squalor in a very uncomfortable Land Rover and not really in tune with all the people in the group. Some didn't believe that cleanliness is next to godliness and spent all the time thinking about where we would spend the night and what we could get to eat. Most were into drugs, even if it was only hash, but it

105

slowed things up a lot and we missed seeing all the really good places as they were beyond our means. We weren't exactly welcome everywhere. I wouldn't use drugs so they laughed at me, and most of them had dysentery or something bordering it."

"Not you?"

"I hate being ill, so I left after the first bout of the runs when I felt terrible." He grinned. "I was a bit more amenable to my family when I returned home and went to college. It was a useful experience in many ways and I was far less anti-social after a few of my mother's wonderful meals and a comfortable bed. I also found I liked learning and enjoyed the lectures."

Penny laughed. "And yet today you are following another very ancient trail of travellers that has very mystical associations." She made the hand signal of the Flower People. "Peace, Brother."

"We shall climb to the top of the Tor and if you have any breath left you can say that again and it will be true. I shall be exhausted and need to meditate."

"Jake would walk up there without stopping," she said wickedly, when the car was parked and they faced the steep winding path up the slope that led to the Tor.

"Aren't you fortunate to have me here? He'd expect you to do it too. I'll let you pause half-way if you are very good and I might even give you some of my chocolate. What would Vincent do?"

"He wouldn't. He'd be appalled at the idea and have to find the nearest bar where he could recover."

"I'm beginning to like Vincent," Chris said as they toiled up the hill that seemed to go on and up for ever. He flung himself down by a moss-covered stone. "What I'd like is a very long Pimms with lots of ice. Don't bother with the cucumber or borage; just the drink."

"Not until you reach the top and go all the way down," she promised maliciously.

"Pull me up."

She bent and held out her hand and he pulled her down beside him, holding her tightly. For a moment she tensed, then laughed and settled into the crook of his arm, her face raised to the sun and the St Christopher medallion swinging over to her shoulder.

"'Breathless we flung us on the windy hill, laughed in the sun and kissed the lovely grass,'" Chris quoted.

"Brooke again? I know him well," she said.

He kissed her, slowly and with tenderness. "Don't waste life, Penny. He goes on to say, 'Heart of my heart, our heaven is now, is won.' He could be right if you'll let it happen."

"I don't know." She turned her face away and he saw that she was close to tears. "We have been together for such a short while and how do we know what the future holds for either of us? I have to go back and see life from that angle again and distance myself from Bath and all I have found there. I'm still confused, Chris, and I could make more mistakes."

"I can wait," he said simply. "I know what I want and I shall not change my mind. If necessary, I'll follow you and make myself a part of your life as a friend, with no pressures, but so that you can't imagine life without me." He smoothed back her hair and she wanted to close her eyes and lose herself in his touch, as her body treacherously told her that she wanted him. "I'm sorry you know the poem." He put a finger on her lips. "Don't say it. It was a bad choice. I had forgotten the last line."

"I have forgotten it too," she lied, but the words throbbed in her brain when he kissed her once more and she didn't know whether to cling to him or to thrust him away. "We

107

laughed and had such brave true things to say . . . and then you suddenly cried and turned away." Don't rush me, it's too soon, she wanted to say but couldn't bear to push him away entirely and hated the thought of him leaving her to find happiness with another woman.

He sat up and brushed the dead grass from his knees. "Do you want to climb to the top?"

"I think we miss the magic if we don't."

"I don't know why I love you."

"Try and think how fit you'll be once you've got there."

"I'm not Jake who climbs anything taller than himself, and I don't have to prove anything."

"Have another piece of rather soft chocolate to give you energy, and follow me!" she said in ringing tones. "Whoops! It does look a bit far up there. I thought we were nearly there. Perhaps we've come far enough."

"You said you wanted to climb, so climb! We can't start life together with a lot of we nearly did this and we tried to do that. What will our children say if they hear that we came here and didn't climb to the top?"

"My children are unborn embryos from Never-Never Land, unlikely to be born," Penny said firmly. "I don't even like children, so if I had some and they sneered at my mountaineering skills I'd be politically incorrect and give them a good slapping."

"I'll remind you of that, one day."

"In any case, I wouldn't want my children to be called Braun. We got over the Helmut crisis but haven't you another last name tucked away somewhere?" She climbed faster when he reached for her and threatened her.

"Didn't you know? My name isn't Braun. My stepmother wanted to keep her own name when she married my father and I was glad she did as it made her seem a very distant relative and not a substitute for my mother. My name is Miller. During the war my father was interned as a prisoner-of-war and met my mother who nursed in the hospital where he was treated after bailing out of his aircraft. He was there for a long time with broken bones and she waited for him until he was released. He was Herr Muller but when he married my mother he changed it by deed poll to Miller – more suitable for a German living in postwar Britain."

"I learn something new all the time."

"With you I am Christopher Miller."

"And in Germany? Are you Helmut Muller?"

"A little, but if you will be with me, I can be anything you like."

"I think we are nearly there," Penny laughed. "Yes, I can see the other side of the hill. I do feel a sense of achievement and that view is fantastic. It's almost worth the effort. Do you believe that this was once surrounded by water and mixed up in the Camelot story? Oh, my aching calves!" She bent down to rub her leg muscles.

"Stay like that." Chris pointed his camera and took three pictures before she could straighten up. Her hair was dishevelled and her shirt was slipping the knot tied in front. Her breasts were gently pushing away the soft fabric, like the Empire gowns she had seen in the museum, half revealing the softness of her bosom. She tugged angrily at the shirt and tied the knot tightly.

Chris grinned and asked another tourist to take a snap of them together, and Penny knew that the prints would indicate that they were very close indeed, in more ways than one.

"You can put me down now," she said primly and held out a hand for the camera. "I must take one of that woman. Do you think she'd object? Her dress and turban are wonderful. Nigerian, would you say?"

"Wait for her to turn round and I think you'll agree that she's British, Kings Road and Carnaby Street."

"So she is! Oh dear, I think she was with the buskers in Bath." She turned to look at the others climbing the Tor.

"He isn't here. I checked back there when I first saw her." Chris smiled in a satisfied way. "I didn't think you would want to see Jake just now."

"Why not? He is my friend."

"Do you want to cope with two men at the same time, both lusting after you? Who knows? We might fight!"

"Stop teasing me and take me down the hill. I need sustenance and that Pimms you suggested sounded like a good idea."

"You may have to slide down on your seat. Dry grass on a slope can be slippery." He held her hand. "That's safer. Trust in me."

She pulled away. "My shoes are fine and I'd rather go alone. Watch it!" She exploded into laughter as Chris slipped and slid twenty yards downhill, landing in an untidy heap. "Want to borrow St Christopher?" She ran down to join him and brushed his shirt. "Trust me," she said and held his hand.

The cafés were full and Penny saw that they catered only for the pizza and burger crowd. Soft ice-cream flowed in spirals from machines and piled high in biscuit cones and the smell of frying onions was stronger than they could face. They walked through the town and found a small pub that served food and cool beer. As it was away from the main road and the crowds, the garden was peaceful. They ordered chicken and salad and crusty rolls and sat under a tall lime tree that smelled sweet, the long stems of blossom rustling in the breeze, almost ready for picking to dry and make lime-flower tea.

Chris pushed back from the wooden table. "We didn't have our Pimms."

"Too late now. It wouldn't go with apple pie and cream." She smiled. "Another time."

"Promise me there will be another time."

"Of course. It's been a wonderful day."

"Promise! Once you go back to London I might lose you."

"I want to keep in touch and I promise that we shall meet again after I get back to London. But you might not be there for very long if your work takes you abroad again, and, according to my manager, I may have to go to Paris soon and maybe to Italy."

"Not to mention Sweden, if Gertrude has her way?"

"That's possible."

"I have an open invitation to visit them."

Penny shrugged. "So have I. What a coincidence."

They laughed and went back to the car, passing the stalls of dried flowers and herbal mixtures, the books on astrology and gem stones, and the fortune-tellers who seemed to be earning their living easily as prospective clients sat on canvas stools waiting for their turns.

She shook her head when Chris gestured towards one, his eyebrows raised in ironic invitation. "Coward!"

"I had mine done years ago and she said I would work in fashion, so she was right."

"Anything more?"

"I forget."

"Due for a memory refresher?"

"No. I'm confused enough as it is, so let's get back to Bath."

When they were in the car, she said, "You could have had your hand read. Why me and not you?"

"I know what I want and if I can't have it, I don't need

111

to be told in advance. You said go back to Bath. Don't you want to see Wells? I intend keeping you to myself for a whole day, so tell me what we are to do next?"

"I'd like to go back and freshen up and then drive along the river and have supper again in the pub we went to with Gertrude and Lars."

"That's a good idea. Cold cathedrals have their limitations on a fine day and I've lit my candles." He drove slowly in the congested streets, where holidaymakers seemed to think they were immune from accident and walked in the middle of the road, and then faster as soon as the town was behind them. "Promise me if I leave you alone, you will stay in your apartment and not show your nose outside in case a wicked wolf comes after you."

"I promise. Give me time to have a shower and change and I'll be ready by six thirty."

Tomorrow, Jake will leave for New Zealand, she thought as she undressed for a shower. A phone call wishing him *bon voyage* would be friendly. No, not that or he might take it that she had regrets and come haring after her again. She let the warm water soothe her aching limbs and cleanse her body and the scent of the soap she'd bought in the shop in Bath reminded her that she'd not given the package to Jake for him to take home for his mother. "Damn! And I don't even like lavender for myself. Ah, well, Aunt Monica will have a double supply."

At the same moment that the door knocker told her that Chris was ready to collect her, the phone rang.

Quickly she opened the front door so that Chris could come in, then picked up the phone. "Yes?"

"Where do you get to all day?"

"I *am* on holiday, Josie, and I have a date right now, so make it quick."

"Vincent bent the rules and rang me."

"And?"

"He wants you over there now, if not sooner."

"I hope you told him to piss off?"

"It's not as easy as that, ducky. He sold them the idea of you doing some of the dresses for the film and they have offered you a lot of dosh! Think of the publicity. I might have my sewing-machine-shaped swimming pool yet!"

"No! I'm not going to America. I shall be back in London the day after tomorrow and we can talk then."

"Make it tomorrow. I can't take the strain and you need to think this through."

"I'm not going."

"See you tomorrow evening, so stop being so bloody selfish. There are a few others to consider, you know. This is business not sex, and we have no intention of missing this wonderful opportunity."

"Does that mean you've told the others?"

"Sure! I rang everyone on the intercom and the news spread to even the ones on holiday, and they all want to pull out the stops and do whatever terrible shoulder-padded horrors that the film needs." She laughed. "We've all watched it and know what they want, but we might manage to push in a few good numbers to keep our reputation."

"If you've planned it all why don't you go to the States and make the bloody things?"

Josie chuckled. "He must be even better than I imagined for you to get uptight about *work*."

"Who?"

"The guy you are going overboard for."

"I'm not." Penny hoped that Chris had not seen her sudden rush of colour. She took a deep breath. "I'll be there tomorrow evening and please leave me to deal with Vincent."

"Get packed and we'll take an early train," Chris said.

113

"I'll take the hire car back tonight and collect you by taxi for the train at ten tomorrow."

"How do you know there's a train at ten? And what about my supper?"

"I pushed my father and stepmother on that train when they left Bath so I do know." He laughed. "As for supper, do you want Thai or Chinese? I'll bring it back after returning the car."

"There's no need for you to come with me," she began.

"Don't argue."

"I suppose you are already booked into Brown's Hotel with the others?"

"They have no idea when I shall meet them, so I intend booking a room elsewhere for a night or so, unless you want me to move in with you . . . strictly on your terms of course."

She gave him a very old-fashioned look. "Thanks for the offer, but no! I have only one very narrow single couch in my studio, and after eight each morning, people milling about the whole building."

"A pity. It sounds cosy and I'm a really early riser. Chinese? Put on the oven. I hate it half cold."

Ten

It was all too much! Penny rummaged for a handkerchief and found it stuck to a tube of sticky winegums she'd forgotten she'd bought in Bath. She wanted to get off the plane and never see an airport again.

Vincent had sent an airline ticket, Club Class, which meant that he had not paid for it but had obtained it from the film unit; Josie had very efficiently changed it for the day after Penny's arrival in London and everything had gone far too smoothly and fast for comfort.

"Shows they want you," Josie pointed out when Penny looked askance at the expensive ticket. "You're right, Vincent wouldn't spend that much on anyone but himself, so it's bona from the people who matter." She packed the folder with the designs that might be needed for America, originally part of the selection made for an Arab family who loved glitter and dashing colours and which might suit the dark woman who was second female lead. She added notes about plans they had made for their own collections. "Don't neglect our stuff. That's where we'll get our bread and jam if this falls through," she remarked shrewdly. "And don't let the buggers get you down. Stand up for your rights, and a lot of money."

"It's not *me*," Penny wailed. "I don't know anything about the American scene and I hate the thought that Vincent has got this for me. He'll expect tons of gratitude and more."

"Don't you believe it! I think he's using you to bolster his own reputation. Actors like him are good but so are a lot more. They are thick on the ground but good designers are rare. In fact, why do we take it for granted that it was Vincent who alerted the film producer to the wonders of our talents? We have shown in London and Switzerland and France, and the salon is doing well, so *someone* may have seen us and liked what they saw."

"I'll remember that. Thanks, Josie, I wish you could be with me to see off the sharks."

"Take Chris," she suggested.

"You met him once for half an hour when he brought me back and I have been with him a very few times. I can't say that *I* know him, so how can *you* suddenly label him sexy flavour of the month and suitable for me as a lover?"

"He can use my phone to check on you, any time," Josie said with maddening calm. "If Vincent gets stroppy, I'll tell Chris that you are madly in love with him and want me to send him over."

"You don't know where he's staying," Penny laughed. "How can you check with him unless he rings you here?"

"He's staying in that small hotel up the road until he gets another apartment where he can work."

"An apartment in London at this time of the year when the place is spilling over with tourists? Even I've had to camp out in the studio as I can't find what I want. I thought he was to join his father in Brown's Hotel. He's on holiday, not working. He may need to go to Munich or Paris soon, so why do you think he needs a studio here as if he's a fixture?"

"Don't be so scathing. You sound as if you don't want him to know what you're doing or have him work so close to you."

116

"It isn't that. I do like him but I feel that I'm being pressured by a lot of people, including you, and I want to lash out and escape again back to Bath."

She felt tired. What happened to my wide green spaces? Are they an illusion that I shall never find among the greys and browns of everyday life?

"He'll find somewhere," Josie said with conviction. "He's the sort to make people want to help him. Why are you grinning?"

"Nothing." Josie would look blank if she told her how lost he'd seemed when she'd helped him to sort out his stamp money, when he knew as much about English currency and postage as she did.

On the plane she refused champagne and opted for fresh orange juice. The first meal was served and, to her surprise, she was hungry, but she had eaten nothing all day as she had had to work fast to get everything in order before she took the flight to New York.

The crisp linen covers, food trays and napkins were removed, a small pillow was offered for her neck and a soft blanket tempted her to sleep, but her mind was in a whirl. The clothes she had worn in Bath that she would have liked to have with her now were at the cleaners, but she had found and packed a few basic trousers, sweatshirts and blouses, with some smarter garments that she had never worn but which Josie said had a bit of glitz and would suit the film scene more than her svelte linen or silk shifts. She hoped she had enough underwear.

"You'll have to learn to sell yourself, as well as showing the gowns," Josie had said. "Take some high heels and strappy sandals and really good tights."

"You make me sound like a prostitute," was her waspish reply, and now, making a mental list of what she had brought, she wondered if one of the dresses was a bit over the top, a far cry from the usually tasteful contents of her wardrobe.

She gulped. There was to be a press call as soon as she had settled after arrival, in a big flashy hotel where she would have dinner with the head of production, the wardrobe director and the script writer, the leading actors . . . and Vincent, who was almost crowing with triumph when he spoke to her on the phone. "Just think what this means to me. I am the only actor apart from the two leading characters to be with you when you meet the press."

Josie had been over-enthusiastic and sent a few sample dresses over as soon as she heard the possibilities. Penny had to admit that they were a good example of what they could produce, but all the same she felt rushed again and hoped that the girls modelling them wouldn't be too blonde, too bosomy or . . . too much.

The seat belt light went on and blankets and pillows were discarded as the passengers tidied up and prepared for landing. Penny carefully put the zippered vanity bag given to Business Class passengers, containing everything that might or might not be needed by a female traveller, in her hand luggage, as she knew that Josie loved to be given such trendy items even if she never used the contents.

Entry into the States was fast and effortless and Penny easily found the driver sent from the studio to take her to the hotel where she would stay for the duration of her visit. She sat back in the car to watch the passing scene of New York City, the crowds who hurried as they did in London, dressed in a similar way, and the yellow cabs that were unfamiliar after the square black cabs she knew so well.

Chris had taken her home in a London cab, insisting on making sure she reached the studio safely with the luggage that had grown during her visit to Bath. That was when he met Josie and, as Josie would say, "clicked" in a way she seldom did with men since her divorce. He had kissed Penny as if to imprint his personality on her memory, so that she would not forget him, and tried to assess her feelings for him, then in an endearing off-hand way, he had offered her his help in anything she wanted from him, even into having his hair cut or dyed, or his lifestyle upturned forever, but he put no pressure on her to make promises.

"Love you too," she'd said and her body told her that she meant it, but he couldn't gauge how deep that went, and left her to Josie and packing and early bed.

The hotel lobby was covered with shiny tiles that looked like a skating rink but were, surprisingly, not slippery, and the vast array of flowers in huge vases could almost convince the casual eye that they were real and not silk and plastic. Penny walked across to the reception desk and showed her passport to a girl who had made every effort to have Cindy Doll as her mirror image. She flashed disconcerting smiles of white, even teeth and crimson lipstick as she took details.

"Just married?" she asked archly.

"What makes you think that?"

"Your husband said you would have your unmarried name in your passport." She glanced at a note. "He said he's working until later and will join you then."

"To whom am I supposed to be married?" Penny tried to sound calm. It was a mistake. The girl was confusing her with someone who had a husband waiting for her in the hotel. She smiled wryly. What a shock for the unfortunate man if she arrived in the room and he was waiting for his bride!

The smile flashed again. "We do have a note. He gave us your old name and your new name, Mrs Vincent Selborne. As he booked a double room, he wanted to avoid embarrassing you over the name on your passport. May I on behalf of the staff and management wish you both every happiness."

"He said that? There's been a mistake. I am not married." She ignored the keys dangling before her. "Which room is it?"

"One of our best double rooms with a fine view of the park."

"I have no idea what has been booked for me by the studio, but it isn't a double room. I am here on business and travelling alone. Book a single room for me under my own name, Miss Penelope Wallace. Do it right now as I am tired and need a shower and coffee and if you can not accommodate me, kindly telephone another hotel which can."

The smile faded. "He said—" she began, then saw Penny's taut expression and the muted fury in her eyes. She pressed buttons on a small computer and reached for a fresh keyring. "I know you will like this room," she said sweetly.

"The studio is paying for my expenses here. *My* expenses," she stressed, and a reluctant smile eased the tension. "Maybe you should clarify the situation with their PRO as I have no idea who is paying for the double room."

She signed the register and picked up the keys. The bellboy took her luggage and Penny turned to the girl, who looked bemused. "Please make sure that any calls come to my own room and to no other person. Have a nice day," she said kindly and walked slowly to the elevator. She giggled. I've always wanted to say that before anyone else could get it in. She almost looked forward to seeing Vincent's face when he found that his first little ploy to make her believe that they were stll considered to be lovers had failed.

The room was smart and bright, if you like pictures of orange sunflowers in one alcove and bullrushes in another, with hooded lamps over them as if they were old masters. The bathroom was good, with a businesslike shower and shallow bath, and there were enough freebie beauty products to make Josie smile for a week.

Penny locked her door, relaxed in a warm shower, towelled herself with soft luxurious pale green towels, then wrapped herself in the towelling robe provided by the hotel and lay on the bed with a cup of coffee by her side.

Shall I make more coffee? she thought lazily, and with a childlike delight examined the packs of coffee, tea, herbal teas and chocolate left for her choice. She nibbled a biscuit and made more coffee, reflecting that a luxury hotel had many advantages over a rented apartment like the one in Bath, which had had a dodgy kettle and nothing in the cupboard.

With the radio alarm set to wake her in good time to dress for the press call, the time of which had been given to her in an envelope along with other dates and times when she must report to the film studio, Penny sank into the pillows, with some of the special cucumber cream she had found among the free goodies smoothed over her eyes, and slipped into a light doze.

The alarm shattered her sleep and she heard the sound of her doorknob being turned, but she ignored it.

"Penny?"

She shook out the dress she'd left on the hanger in the steamy shower room and was pleased to see that all creases had dropped out without having to use an iron. She ignored the plaintive voice, then washed away the cucumber cream and decided that it had done nothing that a good wash in cool water couldn't do to make her eyes sparkle. She felt blissfully rested with no discernible jet lag.

The voice called again but with less vehemence and she went on dressing with care. The simple dress and jacket of cream with coffee edging would, Josie said, look good under the television lights, but be elegant and show how well cut British design could be.

It helped that Penny had a good figure and was attractive enough to show off her own designs, and the high-heeled strappy sandals were just right.

Gertrude would be an asset if she designed handbags and scarves and belts for the next collection, but the soft cream calf bag Penny had brought was small enough to blend with the suit without intruding.

The telephone rang and she answered it, just stating the room number. She nodded and thanked reception. The car was waiting to take her to the other hotel for the press call and the dinner.

"Are you the girl who booked me in?" she asked.

"Sure, I remember you."

"Please page my friend and tell him that he is wanted in his room right away."

"He'll be so pleased to know that. He thought he'd missed you."

"His room, not mine," Penny added, and walked down the three flights of stairs, waiting until she heard his name being called before she ventured into the lobby in time to see him take the elevator upwards.

The car was at the door under the pseudo-Doric columns and the driver smiled and asked if she was alone. "Rather thought there'd be two of you."

"Just me for now." She relented. "Call back again after you've left me, but I have to be there fast."

"Yes, ma'am." He eyed her with approval. "You in this programme?"

"No, I design clothes. I don't act."

"Sure is pretty enough." He turned the car skilfully into the line of traffic and they arrived at the hotel with time to spare before the interviews.

A clone of the girl in the other hotel smiled and ushered her into a large room bristling with microphones. She recognised the leading man from the soap and he smiled. "You are Penny? Just call me Hector. Nice to meet you." He regarded her dress with interest. "One of yours?" She nodded. "We need a bit more class like that," he said, and laughed. "I not only play in it but I have a load of shares, which gives me a lot of muscle when it comes decision-wise. I wanted to be here to see you. They try to keep me away and tell me to keep to my acting, but I have to see what they are doing. The last lot of clothes was crap," he said mildly. "Frankly, when Vince told us he knew you very well, after your name came up as a possibility when we were in congress, I thought that it was a nice bit of nepotism for his girl, but I was mistaken. I saw the things you sent us and they are good. We shall parade them for the press tonight and you shall talk us through." He gave her a wide smile and she saw just what made thousands of female hearts flutter.

"You are staying?"

"Of course." He laughed. "I like to stir things. By tomorrow, the press will be convinced that you are my latest. Hope you don't mind, but Vince will be mad. He says you are an item, but any rumour is good for the publicity of the production so don't let it worry you, unless we want it for real. I think that could be arranged." His smile was lazy and confident and Penny saw red lights flashing in her mind.

"When did you hear about me?"

"You probably don't recall a very awkward customer in your London salon? If I know Karen Bruce, she'd have lifted every hem and examined every seam and tugged at the buttons before she decided on anything. She was impressed in spite of being offered no discount. She said you had never heard of her!" He gave a low whistle. "You'll say now that you never see the soap and never ever read the credits with her name at the top of the production list, after the boss."

"I didn't watch until recently, but I heard the script when Vincent was rehearsing for the audition, and there was no list of director and production teams on that." She wrinkled her nose. "Karen Bruce? I do remember her."

"Made her presence felt?" He seemed amused.

"Sent my head fitter straight up the wall. She wanted a slim gown that would make her pear-shaped hips disappear," Penny said dryly. "But that's what they all want, and we try to meet the challenge. She did buy two dresses, if I remember rightly, and grumbled at the cost."

"That's Karen! She was delighted with them and suggested we contact you for the next series."

Penny shook her head in disbelief. "You could have fooled me. I half expected her to send them back and ask for a refund after she'd worn them!"

"Are people that crass? Well she's here tonight, so you can charm her again. Nice talking to you, Penny. The hyenas are gathering and we must look pleased to see them."

"Thanks for putting me in the picture."

He rolled his eyes in a dramatic way. "You ain't heard nothing yet, Lady. We must get together for the real dirt. C'mon, I'll introduce you to the people who count."

He seized her hand and led her to the rostrum where a group of people were gathered. After five minutes she was confused, but thought that if she called half the men Si, and the other half Bud, she'd get a few right. Karen Bruce was dressed elegantly, and Penny approved. And why not, as the dress was one that she recognised as hers?

It was obvious that any detail to do with the soap was news and there was even an audience of invited guests to watch the interviews and hear hints of the joys to come in the next series.

Green Spaces

At last Penny was introduced and she wanted to giggle when the compere made her sound like Christian Dior, Ungaro and Chanel rolled into one. She watched the faces in the audience and saw that they seemed to believe every word. I'll have to be careful what I say and do here. She thought of some of the off-hand and mildly insulting jibes that passed for humour and even affection in her workrooms and of Josie's outspoken comments when she disliked a client. Here, she knew instinctively that everything might be taken down and used in evidence!

Hector, or Lance Reaval as he was known professionally, said a few flattering words that made the camera crew laugh and eye her with speculation, and she knew that she must be careful who she trusted. Her mother had once said, "Who gossips to you will gossip about you," and it might be true here.

The models wafted along the brightly lit catwalk and showed the gowns and outfits to perfection. Penny made the commentary brief, but added that this was just a selection from her salon in London and other garments would of course be designed and adapted to what was needed for the individual stars, a task to which she looked forward with great anticipation.

Cameras clicked and many of the audience made a note of the London salon. Josie would be proud of me, she thought, and was amused by the whole extravagant set-up.

The PRO urged them to go to the dining-room annexe, a high atrium that resembled a rain forest with luscious vegetation and exotic flowers, where drinks were offered and small talk exchanged, under the ever-present eyes of the gossip columnists.

Penny half listened to the talk and heard that the leading lady was having an affair with one of the technicians, not the wealthy financier that the gossips had labelled her property. This titbit was told in a half-whisper that could have reached reception, with a look towards the columnist of *Vogue Colourada*.

"Another reputation dented," Hector said softly.

"Is it always like this?"

"No, they are a bit on edge tonight. There's to be a reshuffle of female actors with the introduction of two new characters. No hassle for the cast as nobody loses a part but they are paranoic at times and get bitchy, wondering if the axe will fall." He turned away but held her hand. "Hi, Mark. Whadya think?" The cameraman smirked and as Hector kissed her cheek, she knew that her picture would be in at least one periodical in the morning showing her in intimate contact with the leading actor.

She smiled weakly and wished she was miles away. It was almost a relief to see Vincent hurrying towards her, looking very smart but flustered. He forced a smile and said hallo, but was put off by seeing the most important man in the company holding Penny by the hand.

"Hallo, Vincent," she said in a flat voice, then looked up at Hector. "I'd like a word with Karen. She looks so good in that dress and I must thank her for bringing me here."

Even his ears were red, and Vincent looked deflated. He hadn't bargained on her finding out so soon that she had not needed him to get this assignment. "See you later," he said in a low voice. "We must talk, darling."

"Of course. See you in the hotel lounge after this is over. We can have a drink before I go to my nice single room."

"Penny?"

"Not now, Vincent. I must talk to Karen before we are shown to our tables."

Eleven

The illusion of being on the other side of a glass panel watching a play persisted through the meal. The faces of her companions were carefully made-up, even the men seemed to have enhanced eyebrows and . . . yes, some lips were discreetly outlined. Two women had tightly achieved smoothness after cosmetic surgery, giving a doll-like look and a lack of expression.

Each time a camera light flashed, Penny seemed to be laughing at something Hector was saying, or he was looking at her over a wineglass in what could only be called a "meaningful" way, until she suspected that he had his own private photographer who would convey to the public just what Hector wanted him to.

Vincent made a great show of entertaining the second female lead, a type that Penny recalled he hadn't admired when he met her on the yacht. He'd hinted that she was too Carmen Miranda, too pushy and had a habit of stealing the limelight from any other actor in the room, but now she was well-known her personality did have its advantages. He had the satisfaction of being included in the many photographs that the indefatigable snappers took.

However, from time to time he stared across at Penny, and she could feel his anger, fear and frustration when he saw her being absorbed into the upper echelons of the production unit and observed that Hector had designs on the designer he considered was his own property.

At last the meal was over, people drifted out to the bar and Penny stifled a yawn, the events of the past day and night catching up on her.

"Bushed?" Hector asked.

"A bit," she admitted. "I'll see you tomorrow."

"I'll drive you," he said, but the producer called to him and Vincent came over and slipped into his place.

"Penny and I are together," Vincent called. "I'll see her home."

Hector nodded, raised a practised eyebrow, shrugged and turned away, and Penny found herself in a cab with the man who wouldn't take no for an answer. He tried to hold her hand but she drew away sharply. "Stop right there, Vincent. You had no right to book me in with you." She gave a short laugh. "Newly weds? What did you think? I'd say nothing and move in with you, after you know we broke up for good?"

"We didn't break up for ever. It was a blip in our relationship. I asked you to marry me, didn't I?" he sounded hurt.

"And I said no and meant it. I might have felt a little bit grateful if you'd really worked at getting me this contract, but even that was a lie. It was Karen who suggested me, and you tagged on to the idea and set me up for this trip as if I was joining you so that we could be together." She glared, and he wished that the space between them was greater. He had forgotten what she was like in a temper – he had encountered her wrath so seldom in the past when life was simple and even a trifle humdrum.

"What's got into you, Penny? Must be jet lag," he said kindly, in the irritating tone he used when he would say, "it must be the time of the month," if she didn't agree with him. "You aren't like this. Were you upset by Hector? He makes passes at every new female he meets. It means nothing, but you need me to keep men like him away as I did in the past."

"I'm beginning to think that you kept away a lot of very nice people just to make sure I stayed with you. I thought you had my best interests at heart but now I know better. I've been around a lot more since we split up and I've met some very interesting men. I may marry one of them," she added defiantly.

The cab stopped and the driver grinned as she left Vincent to pay and stormed into the hotel foyer. "Room three hundred and fifty-four," she said and took the key of her room. At least that was settled.

"Don't go," Vincent said as he hurried after her. "Let's have a drink in the lounge."

She looked at his desperate expression and was slightly moved that he was showing genuine emotion which she thought had nothing to do with the advancement of his career. "Coffee," she conceded and glanced at her watch. "Half an hour, as I must get to bed. Karen suggested a meeting at nine thirty and I have to get my notes together."

"I have an early start, too." Vincent made it sound as if his meeting was far more important. "We have a very tricky scene to film and I was hoping you'd hear my lines."

Penny left her coffee untouched and stared. "You really did think I'd come here and we'd be the same as we were before we broke up for good!"

"We were made for each other. Nothing that has happened will ever make any difference. We are as one, and deep down you know it as well as I do."

Two guests seated on an adjoining settle turned to listen when she laughed aloud. "Vincent, this is *me*. I heard those lines when we went through the script and I thought them corny even for this stupid soap!"

"Even clichés start out as truth," he said stiffly. "Those words happen to be what I feel. I love you, Penny, and it's time you came to your senses and married me."

She got up and smoothed down her skirt. She sounded tired. "Don't you ever give up? I have to phone Josie. What is the time difference?"

"I've no idea, but it will do that bitch good to be woken in the middle of the night," he said bitterly. "I hold her responsible for a lot of our troubles. She never liked me."

"I have great respect for her taste." Penny tried to smile. "Let's not quarrel. We shall see a lot of each other if I work over here for a while and we can be good friends."

He smiled, hopefully. "Stop this rubbish of having a single room. Apart from being embarrassing for me, it's so silly. Come to bed now, darling. We can start over again."

She counted up to five, then gave him an icy smile, her hands clenched as if she wanted to hit him. "You haven't listened to a word I said." She turned away but her words were still audible to the fascinated neighbours who had abandoned their attempts at small talk and listened avidly. "Even sleeping together is impossible, Vincent. I am no longer on the Pill and I shudder to remember your attempts at condom control!" She hurried to the elevator.

How could I? What kind of a bitch am I? Her cheeks were hot and she almost returned to apologise, but the elevator took her up relentlessly and she was faced with the door of her own room and the moment passed. Vincent would have been understanding, forgiving and . . . triumphant.

The telephone purred for her attention. "Miss Wallace?" The receptionist seemed relieved. "I'm glad I found you. I tried the other room first and there was no answer."

She interrupted, and if the girl could have seen her, she'd have felt like ducking out of range of Penny's wrath. "What other room? My room is three-five-four."

The girl giggled. "We all know that you aren't married and you personally booked a separate room, but we understood from Mr Selborne that you were really together. We are *very* discreet. The girl who was on duty earlier told me all about you."

"My room is three-five-four. I have no idea what number Mr Selborne is using and I have no intention of visiting him there. Is that understood? I am here on business and I have no time to waste on acquaintances who try to get into my knickers! The hotel should be trying to protect women guests from men like that, instead of aiding them."

"I'm sorry, really sorry." The girl was confused, upset, and coughed to hide her embarrassment. "You have a call, Miss Wallace. Mr Lance Reaval is on the line and wants to come over if you are here."

"Who?"

"The leading man in 'The Smiling Lake Saga'," the girl almost bleated. "Oh dear, I think of him as Lance, but that's his stage name."

"I met him at the press conference," Penny said slowly. "We shall meet again on the set tomorrow, so unless he has urgent business to discuss in the lounge downstairs, I am very tired after flying from UK, and I think it would be best if you said you can't locate me."

"You kidding?"

"No, anything but that! I am quite normal, but I am very tired and want no more social contacts tonight. I think that Hector is a fine actor, I like men, I have a boyfriend at home and I am here to do a good job, if possible. No more calls tonight please."

Penny turned out the box in her case that contained various items that could easily be mislaid and found the gadget that Josie had insisted that she use in all big hotels in New York or Los Angeles. It had seemed amusing at the time but now Penny fitted the anti-intruder additional lock to her door, put on the safety chain and went to bed feeling under siege.

On impulse, she rang for room service and ordered breakfast in her room for the following morning, then cancelled it. "I'm going crazy! If I breakfast alone up here, they'll think I have a man with me, and if I go down to eat, I shall risk seeing Vincent again and that's too soon."

She rose early to avoid Vincent and after breakfast in the sun-room, alone at a single-seat table and waited on with care as if everyone had been warned about the bad-tempered English designer, life seemed normal and Penny looked forward to an interesting day. She paused by reception where the original girl was on duty again and handed her a note of all the people she would speak to on the telephone if she was in the hotel, which included Josie, her fabric designer, a couple of women friends and as an afterthought, although it was unlikely that he would try to contact her, Christopher Miller.

Sorry, Chris, she thought. I have to show that I have a boyfriend in England and you are conveniently available.

The girl scrutinised the list. "You haven't included any of the film people?"

"Sorry. Add Karen Bruce and the producer whose name escapes me but I'm sure you know it as you're such a fan of the series."

"I have here a note that Lance Reaval rang last night." Just mentioning his name seemed to give her a thrill.

"That's right. I said I was unavailable and he is not on the list. I don't often mix business with pleasure and I shall see him on the film set."

"Most women would give anything to date him. He is just gorgeous." The girl sighed.

"You haven't seen my boyfriend in England," Penny said

and hoped her smile was light and knowing. Poor Chris! What would he think?

"He must be quite something!"

"He is. Has my car arrived? It's time I left."

Penny thought back to the time when the house was cleared and everyone parted for fresh fields. Talk about clearing the attic! She had scrubbed away the detritus of years and now she had resisted three men in the past month, or four if she counted the resumed efforts of Vincent. She included Hector as she was sure that he didn't pay calls at nearly midnight unless he wanted a bed for the night.

All this with no sex and a firm resistance to offered real love, if it existed. She smiled wryly. More men than I can cope with and no satisfaction. No rest in my green spaces of calm, as my mind is in perpetual turmoil.

Penny showed her pass to the chunky doorman guarding the gate and the car swept through the entrance to the film set. Karen Bruce met her at the door of the small office allotted to the designer team and led her out of another door at the back where a large room with long tables and many cupboards and changing cubicles was ready for work.

"It was agreed that my studio in London would make the garments after they receive the toiles," Penny said firmly.

Karen nodded reluctantly. "Don't you think it more convenient to have our girls working on the spot or to offload some to another firm?"

"No. My staff know exactly what I want and I have read the contract carefully. I think I'll need one of my seamstresses here who will check the toiles and send them back to London with a full explanation of what is to be done. The garments I brought with me may be copied in other fabrics here if necessary, but the logo of my firm remains on every garment, exclusively."

"Sure," Karen sighed. "I'd hoped—" she began, then

saw Penny's expression and shrugged. "God save me from women who read the small print, but I confess I like to know where we stand from the beginning. I know we can agree on the stuff we need." She smiled. "Nothing in the agreement to stop you making a little something for me, is there?"

"When I've finished the first batch I can take time off to do my own thing."

"I know! It's in the contract that you have two weeks off every two months." Karen gave a shrug of resignation.

"I can see that you too have read the small print," Penny replied and sensed a fresh business respect growing between them. "My manager did include a few finished models that I had sent over and she reminded me that some would fit the measurements we had for you when you bought from us in London. I am under contract to the film company to design for a session here but my salon in London will go on making clothes as usual, so anything you want can be ordered from them direct."

"When can I see the ones you brought with you? Why don't we have lunch and have a fitting at your hotel?"

"Any time you say, but later, Karen. I have the models here ready for fitting. This morning we have sketches to discuss and work to put in hand."

Josie would never believe that I could be so firm, Penny thought, with a feeling of satisfaction, and it was a shock to find that the morning had gone quickly and smoothly and Karen was waiting with the car to take her back to the hotel.

"Later we'll see the rushes of the morning's shots and you can see what they wore for the cocktail party. We used two of your dresses and I think they'll have to modify some of the others as they look a bit over the top, even for this shower. Hector was right. He hated the last designer collection and your frocks show a bit of class."

"May I give you lunch here?" asked Penny when Karen followed her into the hotel lobby as if she meant to stay.

"Why not in your room? We can combine lunch with a fitting."

"Sorry, I did say I had the dresses in the fitting rooms back at the film set. There really isn't space for them in my room and we can ask the machinist to be on hand to make any alterations. We may need to press some that were packed." She smiled. "The smaller dining-room is quiet and pleasant and we can talk there."

Karen looked annoyed. "Surely you have at least one here that I can fit on?"

"I made a resolution to keep work away from wherever I stay or I'd be up half the night checking seams and thinking about alterations to the designs. It's better to keep that side of my life in a separate compartment, and there is a security risk in big hotels which could affect insurance, or so I was told."

"OK," Karen said in a flat voice. "Later, but I hope we can be real close over this project."

"I hope so too. Everyone has been most welcoming," Penny replied politely and wondered why the woman repelled her now that they were not working.

"Hector of course will try his darndest to get you into bed and Vincent looks like a puppy who was kicked in the balls whenever you're around." She smiled as if the idea gave her pleasure. "Men! Who needs them?"

"A time and a place for everything," Penny said lightly. "I work mostly with women and we get on fine. My manager Josie is very efficient and a good friend, but men do have their uses."

"Vincent gave us all to believe that you were his property, but it's rumoured that you booked a separate room."

"Quite an efficient grapevine! We lived together in

135

London but that's over and we can now be just good friends," Penny asserted crisply.

"So you found him unsatisfying, and now are . . . free?"

The hairs at the back of Penny's neck seemed to crawl, and she noticed for the first time that Karen's eyes were hooded and calculating. She looked like one of Penny's girls, who had left the salon in London after complaints from clients that she was too familiar when fitting garments, and now lived with a rich woman who made no secret of the fact that she cruised the singles bars.

"I'll have soup and a salad," she said to the waitress. "And plain mineral water." No alcohol until dinner and then only a glass of wine, she told herself. I'm going to need all my wits about me here. She bent over her soup and hoped she could control the urge to laugh hysterically. What is happening to me? I am the same woman who lived in London and had to cope only with Vincent and my work, but now I am working in a high-powered situation and, as my Aunt Monica would say, I'm a veritable honeypot, and if I read the signs correctly, not only for men!

Karen pushed her chilli round her plate and looked at her watch. "I oughter get back. See you at three, honey." Briefly, she touched Penny on the shoulder and picked up her purse. "Later?"

"I'll make sure they are all there ready for you."

As Karen left, the receptionist came over. "I know he isn't on your list but Lance Reaval is on the telephone and wants to know if you are lunching here. You *are*, so what do I say?"

Penny smiled sweetly. "Tell him that I am having a business lunch with Karen Bruce in the small dining-room. We have got to the coffee stage if he likes to join us." She saw the girl look at the empty chair. "She's in the john but she'll be back. Let me know if he's joining us."

The coffee was strong and fragrant. Penny had a feeling that she would need to drink a lot of it while in the States. The girl came back, disappointed with the message that Hector would catch up with Miss Wallace on the set after lunch. Penny giggled and wondered if he'd ever tried to get Karen into bed.

She freshened up in her room and selected a few more sketches, as Karen had hinted that more silk suits would be needed for a big hotel luncheon scene when the hero would make a speech before a crowd of fashionably dressed extras. Obviously money was no problem, and the backers had every confidence that money well spent up front would bring in the bacon.

She examined the list of suggestions, which included the fact that the producer wanted a few elegantly attired larger women to be included in each crowd scene, to make overweight viewers feel that they too could fantasise about looking glamorous.

"Good psychology," she murmured and found four sketches for the plump wife of an Arab sheikh that had never been made up because he had insisted that she gave up Western dress during a religious crisis in his country. Poor soul, to spend her life in shapeless black, Penny thought and remembered the pleasure the lady had had in wearing well-cut suits and dresses and the floaty chiffon trousers that pared off her rounded hips.

Karen was brisk and businesslike and Penny enjoyed working with her. They watched the rushes and a lot of stills taken of previous episodes and it was clear that the new designs had the edge on fashion over the rather fussy gowns worn earlier.

The star of the soap came for measuring and saw the sketches of her future dresses. Penny made a note that pastels and clear bright colours would suit the natural blonde with the wide blue eyes and size eight figure. A pale lavender velvet with deep purple trim would be unusual and subtle and totally devastating if used for an evening gown with a boned bustier and softly draped chiffon stole. The fine muslin toile, that would be the pattern for the garment, was made to fit exactly before precious material was cut. It took shape, and work began in earnest.

"Is Clarrie your real name?" Penny asked.

"Sure." The girl pouted. "I wanted to be called Kylie but they said there were enough in films already and Clarrie would do nicely." She picked up a sketch. "This one is a real darlin'. My contract says that I can keep two outfits from each series and this will be one. I didn't bother with the last lot as they were crap." She gave a wicked smile. "I did take them but sold them to a fan who just loved them. I wouldn't be seen dead in them off stage. Just because I'm a blonde they thought I must have girly frills."

"My manager Josie suggested the colours to suit you as she watched the last series and she was right. Nothing dark or heavy and plenty of softness."

"You can keep the Hispanics for Pilar. She looks great in them but they would kill me," Clarrie admitted. "It's great to see that you know the difference."

Penny nodded and adjusted a pleat. Pilar, the Spanish-looking second lead, was quite different and she wondered if Vincent had got any further than a dinner-table flirtation with her. Serve him right if he has, she thought maliciously. She'd eat him whole for breakfast. Why does she remind me of a black widow spider?

"What's funny?" Karen asked.

"Just remembered that Clarrie had to wear that ethnic skirt and obviously hated it," she lied.

"I have to see the producer," Karen said. "I'll be back in half an hour to have my fittings."

Clarrie watched her leave and giggled. "Take care, Penny."

"Why?" Penny looked up from the hem she was tacking. Clarrie looked too innocent. "Why do you say that?" she repeated.

"Didn't take her five minutes to get her clothes off for you."

"I brought several things that will suit her if she wants them."

"Harriet," Clarrie called to the girl who was folding a spare roll of muslin. "Stay with Penny. Our friendly little Karen is having fittings and Penny is sure going to need you."

Twelve

"Lovely to hear your voice." Penny sank back in the soft chair and relaxed.

"It can't be as bad as that!" Josie laughed. "Are they all too much?"

"Not all," Penny replied. "And I've been very firm about my contract, the fabrics I need and the fact that the work is not to be farmed out to another firm that wants to have its name on the credits."

"Good girl. How is Vincent? Must be hopping mad."

"Just a little, but getting the message at last. I haven't seen him for three days. Why ask about him?"

"He must have seen the pictures? They were published yesterday in the weeklies. How can you be so laid back about them?"

"What pictures?" Penny felt suddenly tense with foreboding.

"From all those in the magazines it seems that you are a very busy girl." Josie's voice went up an octave. "You really haven't seen them? Really truly?" She gave a snort of disgust. "Rather you than me, even if he has such a wonderful sexy body. Be careful in bed. With his reputation you don't know where he's been."

Penny sat up. "What do you mean? Who are we talking about?" She heard the rustle of paper.

"Nice one at the table and another when he said hallo and

kissed your cheek. One thing in his favour: he makes you laugh. There are loads of other pictures. The article was a bit much, I thought."

"Do you mind telling me what this is about? I have been here for just over two weeks now, I am not sleeping with anyone, I am eating well and not drinking more than a glass of wine at dinner and I am not into drugs. I don't even walk to work and I haven't been mugged. The work is fascinating and the girls are great."

"And Lance? Is he as great in all departments as rumour has it?"

"What magazines?"

Josie told her three names and Penny groaned. "I thought he had a pet photographer who followed him everywhere but I didn't think it went that far. It's a set-up. I've been careful not to invite anyone back here. *Not anyone*! He has tried to date me but I know he does that to all the new women."

"*Ahem*! Listen to this, and I quote. 'Mr Lance Reaval, the star of your favourite soap, confessed to our reporter that he is madly in love and although he would say nothing about the lucky lady, which is strange as he isn't usually so coy, we do have some very interesting pictures. American women, eat your hearts out.' Do I go on?"

"No, I'll send down for the magazines. I'm getting used to some very funny looks here from the hotel staff since I booked a single room and gave Vincent the elbow, but this is new. *Help!*"

"Wish I could, but we are very, very busy, taking on extra staff as the word has spread and we are flavour of the month in at least two fashion mags . . . one with your picture, ducky, and that article. Lots of orders. That's the good news."

"That's good. What's bad?"

"Chris came by and asked about you."

"That's bad?"

"If you want that guy, be positive. He saw the pictures and you *do* look very friendly."

"He wouldn't believe that tripe."

"Why not?" Josie said calmly. "He's a man and he's in love with you." She chuckled. "At first glance even I believed it, then dismissed it as a giggle, but I'm not in love with you. He's off to Paris next week. Do I tell him to pop over the pond first?" She became serious. "I'd tell him if I was sure you really wanted him but he's too damned decent to play with and use for a safety net. He makes lizards like Lance look like trash."

"I just don't know." The words were wrung from her. "Tell him . . . oh what's the use? Tell him I'm wearing St Christopher to protect me from lying reporters. Tell him . . . no, forget it, and send me a nice chaperone who can sew. We have to do some work over here and not send it all back to you if they want it soonest."

Josie chuckled. "Like Liz?"

Penny visualised the earnest hard-working girl with the no-nonsense jaw, nice eyes and wide hips. She laughed weakly. "Just who I need. I really do like her and she deserves a break. Pack her up with the sketches and send her over. Better call it a holiday until we get her work permit sorted."

"St Christopher is for travellers not protection. Choose another saint, ducky. You aren't going anywhere now we are on a wave, so don't even think of running away."

"I could go to New Zealand. It's soft and green there. It's peaceful and I could learn to make scones and count sheep."

"Silly cow," Josie said comfortably. "You're the green one if you think the Kiwi is the answer, but I've sent on a letter from him and one from Sweden, though I kept the package she sent as you said you were expecting samples of rainproof scarves."

"Look at them and see what you think. I like the Swedes as friends but you will be more objective, so you can deal with it."

"I already peeped and they're great. I'll place an order today and ask for the contact who sells the material so that we can make a pilot selection of raincoats. I've chosen my freebie. If the rain doesn't stop, I'll try it today. It might be the answer to soggy hair."

"This call is costing a fortune. I'll ring you tomorrow and the studio can pay. Take care."

"No, *you* take care. I'll send in the cavalry as soon as I get transport settled for Liz."

The in-house phone purred just as Penny approached it. "Yes," she said abruptly.

"Flowers arrived for you, Miss Wallace, and . . ."

"Well, send them up. Is that all?" She sensed that the girl had more to say.

"A representative of the press would like to interview you and offered to bring the flowers at the same time."

"I made it clear in my original hand-out that any interviews about the collection would take place at the studio. I'd prefer it if the bellboy left the flowers outside my door and knocked briefly. I'll take them in at my leisure."

"The flowers are from Lance Reaval," the girl said reverently.

"I see. They can go now to my studio instead of up here. It needs some flowers. Pop them in a taxi and tell the driver to deliver them to Karen Bruce for the studio. I don't like flowers in my personal rooms," she lied. "They don't go with air-conditioning. Give me a buzz when the car is here to take me to the meeting. Any interviews can be conducted on the set if they are concerned with my work."

She glanced at her watch and picked up the pale lemon suede jacket that matched her slim skirt. Her purse was a deeper shade of buttercup and the St Christopher medallion hung outside the ice-blue shirt as if to show the world that she was under a kind of divine protection. Some women wear a cross, she thought, but the memory of the physical Christopher at that moment was more powerful and comforting than any emblem. Her briefcase was ready and she had ten minutes to spare before the car arrived. She left the room quietly, glancing along the corridor before running down the stairs.

The side entrance leading to the rank of shops made for an easy getaway, and Penny bought the magazines that Josie had suggested before turning back and following the sidewalk to the front of the hotel where her car was easing up to the domed pillars at the main entrance. She hurried to catch the driver before he entered the building and he recognised her. "Went shopping," she explained with a bright smile. "Let's go."

Half-way to the studio she took out her mobile phone and rang the hotel reception. "Miss Wallace had a change of plan and has already left for the studio," she said briskly, and cut short the puzzled voice of the girl at the desk.

She glanced at one magazine and hated what she saw. Every picture showed a laughing intimacy with Hector, and there was no mistaking the light in his eyes. Did she imagine it or did the driver look at her with calculating interest when she left the car?

"Seen the pics?" Karen looked sour.

"You were there all the time. You know it wasn't like they make out, Karen!"

"I hope not. Let's get on. They need another suit for our little blonde bombshell, so can we glance at some sketches? You'll have to have this made over here as it's urgent."

"No problem with rush jobs in future," Penny replied as calmly as she could. "One of my best girls is on her way over and she can cope with them if she has another girl to do exactly as she tells her."

"Great. You do need extra skilled hands." Karen managed a smile. "You'd be wasted on him. Just watch your back, honey. He can't get into bed with Clarrie as she's stuck on one of the lighting engineers, and he thinks he needs publicity for the great loverboy image just now to keep up the ratings. Guess what? He has a financial interest in two of the mags and they set up his stories."

"When Liz arrives, where can I find accommodation for her?"

"There's a hostel where a lot of the workforce live, but if she's not into communal living she can use a wagon in the trailer park at the back of the set until she finds something. I'll fix it if you want that. What's she like?" Karen asked casually. "Boyfriend?"

"I doubt it. She works hard and spends her spare time with her sister who has four children."

"I look forward to meeting her. It sounds as if she needs some fun." She moved away to compare two fabric swatches.

"Not that kind of fun," whispered Pat, who was tacking a hem at the table where Karen and Penny had been talking. She straightened up and saw that Karen had left. "She was real mean when she saw your pictures."

"I can't think why. She was at that dinner and saw everything."

"What was he like, really truly, when you were alone with him?"

"As I haven't been alone with him at the studio and he's certainly never visited me in the hotel, I wouldn't know. I suppose what you see is what you get, a rather spectacular-looking guy with a lot of charm and even more vanity."

Pat glanced towards the door. "It might be better if you did date him or the spider may try for you."

"I try to convince everyone that I have a boyfriend but nobody listens. I'm here to work and to enjoy all the lovely perks, not to sleep around with anyone."

"Cool it. It was a friendly warning." Pat grinned. "You're doing fine and if you want a minder for your new girl, let me know. I live in one of the trailers. I can keep an eye on her."

"Thank you. I really appreciate that." Penny cast her mind back to Liz when she first saw her being interviewed by Josie. Nervous, but sure of her own worth as a couturier assistant, she had produced examples of her work, unlike two other interviewees who seemed to think that a bold manner and a touch of glamour would get them jobs anywhere, even if their past achievements were sketchy.

"She'll do," Josie had said, which meant that she was very impressed, and Liz was now the best girl in the salon and workshop.

"Liz will need a friend," Penny said slowly. "She looks as if she can handle any situation and she can, as far as work goes, but she hasn't had much experience of the big outside world and this set-up will be very strange."

"Discos? Boyfriends?" Pat looked hopeful. "Now I've finished with Mike I need someone to tag along with and she might enjoy a night out."

"Liz is quiet and I doubt if she's ever been to a disco. She isn't exactly pretty but she's very nice."

"Ah well, I'll still take her under my wing," Pat replied cheerfully. "No problem and no competition!"

Work was going well and ideas came easily in the peace of the huge studio. When Pat folded the protective sheet over the plastic figure wearing the last toile pattern, it was a shock to see how late it was.

"I'd no idea of the time. You should have said it was long past the time for you to leave, Pat."

"I've been having a ball. It's good to work quietly and to see it coming together so well." She turned down the corners of her mouth. "Shit! It *is* late and the canteen will be closed. They aren't shooting tonight so they close the food trailer and send everyone home."

"Can you cook in your trailer?"

"If I'm desperate, but desperate. You haven't tasted my cooking or you wouldn't ask. I'll go along to the deli." She sighed. "Bagels again or stuffed pitta and I'm trying to lose weight."

"I'm starving, so why not let me buy you dinner at the diner by my hotel? I hate eating out alone and I don't want to be in my room or the restaurant in the hotel this evening until much later, to avoid the press if they are still baying at my door." She saw that Pat was uncertain. "Really, you'd be doing me a favour."

"Let's go then and thanks. I need food."

They ordered steaks and salad and red wine and ate in near silence until the last of the salad had disappeared, then talked of their work, the people and a little of their own personal backgrounds. Pat giggled. "Karen was so funny. She tried to send me and Harriet off on messages while you fitted her with the clothes you brought over, but we acted dumb and one stayed if the other was away."

Penny smiled faintly. "She's very good at her job and I respect her for that but if she wants anything more, it takes two to tango, and that isn't my dance."

"You played it right and I think she will be easy now. Nice lady in many ways but unhappy."

"That's the impression I get. More coffee?"

"No, I'll be off now. I can catch a bus outside your hotel, so I don't have to walk far."

Penny went into the foyer cautiously. It was very late and the place was quiet.

"Any messages?" she asked when she was given her key.

"Mr Lance Reaval rang twice, a fax came from London, England, and there was another call from a guy called Miller." The girl saw Penny blush. "He rang twice," she said, as if very impressed.

"Mr Miller rang twice?"

"No, Mr Reaval of course. He wants you to ring him tonight as he wants to see you. I can tell him that you have returned."

"What time did Mr Miller ring?"

The girl cast an uninterested glance at the memo. "About nine."

"Did he leave a message."

"Sounded a bit of a cookie."

"What did he say?"

Adopting an air of faint displeasure, the girl read from the memo. "Caller said that he had your message from Josie and was glad that St Christopher was with you. Didn't make sense."

"Oh yes it did." Penny's face glowed.

"Do I connect you with Mr Reaval? I think he does want to come over." Her hand hovered over the phone.

"Who? Oh, no, it's far too late and I shall see him on the set tomorrow, so no calls tonight unless it's Mr Miller. Is that the fax from my manager? Thanks, I'll deal with it upstairs. I may need a line to London but I'll let you know." She laughed, suddenly light-hearted at the thought that Chris had rung. "It's so quiet. Everyone asleep or dead? At least I'm not faced with that reporter. I hope he sleeps well."

148

The girl gave a strangled cough and reddened.

"What is it? He isn't here now?"

The girl looked towards the lift and twisted a hotel brochure into a tight roll. "I'm not sure. He did go up earlier with Mr Reaval just to look around but Mr Reaval left soon after that."

"And did Mr Reaval have his picture taken going into my room?" she asked icily. "I suppose he did?"

"He said you had a book he wanted, so security let him in for a minute. Only for a minute," she added unhappily.

Even to the girl it sounded a weak excuse, and Penny thought back to a friend who had doctored a picture to put two people together as a joke, as if they were really an item, and she knew how easy it would be to put two pictures together and make it one. It had seemed fun at the time but this was different.

"If I find anything disturbed, I shall leave the hotel tomorrow. If I stay and am not given the privacy promised me here I shall complain to the managing director of the whole hotel chain."

"I'd lose my job!"

"Yes." Penny was adamant. "I rather think you deserve to do so. Do reporters pay you for tip-offs when there is anyone even vaguely newsworthy staying here?"

The girl nodded, her eyes filling with tears.

"Ring for the security officer and tell him that a man is lurking about the corridor close to my room and Miss Wallace refuses to go there until he is removed." She gave a tight smile. "Feel free to say that I am an awkward bitch who has a lot of influence with the film people who put their visitors in this hotel and that I have threatened to complain about the much advertised security here. I also have an aversion to being mugged, mentally or physically. I shall walk up to the first landing and sit there until someone comes to escort me up to my room."

I hope that they believe I have more influence than is true! Penny crossed her fingers and decided that as her name had been linked with Hector she was for a brief time important to the press and the hotel, so this outburst would be taken seriously.

Ten minutes later, a man in uniform approached her where she sat on one of the chairs at a table in an alcove by the middle floor elevator. "He's gone, ma'am. Right out of the building. I'll see you home and look under the bed." His laconic smirk labelled her as a fussy cow.

"Thanks. When I ask to have my room changed tomorrow, please make sure that nobody knows of the change or I'll hold you and the girl downstairs responsible."

"Yes, ma'am." His reply was more placating. "No need to make changes. I'll see you aren't disturbed."

"You surely will," she announced briskly. "I shall have a different room number by noon tomorrow. I hope that the photographer can explain to the next person occupying my old room that Mr Reaval does not visit there, even if his picture appears in a magazine with him entering that numbered door. She or, even worse, *he* might be embarrassed."

The man unlocked her door and switched on the lights. A bottle of champagne and a large vase of flowers were prominently displayed on the telephone table. "Take this rubbish," Penny said angrily. "Give it to the staff here if you can't bear to destroy it." She tore up the small card with the flowers. "Tell reception that I want a line to London right now."

"Your attorney?" he said with alarm.

"Not tonight but I may sue for harassment if I'm not protected." She locked the door carefully, adding Josie's gift to the lock and lifted the phone. Josie would probably be at work now so she could call the office. As always Penny was amazed at the clarity of the line and the swift connection with a place half-way across the world.

"Liz?" she said, when she heard the low voice. "Is Josie there?"

With more enthusiasm Liz told her that she was catching the night plane and would see her soon.

"I'll have a cab waiting for you with your name on a card, so watch out for him."

"Thank goodness. I want to come over but that really bugged me, having to find my way to your place. Josie is here now."

"Hi there, celebrity."

"You can stop that or I'll ring off!" Penny told her of the evening's events and answered a few questions that she had read in the fax. "I had a message from Chris but he said nothing about his trip to Paris."

"Why haven't you written to him?"

"What do I say? I don't know how I feel about him and it isn't fair to want him here just to pretend that I have a boyfriend."

"You could use Vincent for that."

"No way, now he knows I am serious about breaking up. He seems interested in the second female lead and she has dinner with him. Also, he moved out of the hotel so I don't see him very often."

"I have an address in Paris. Make a note right now and write to him. He'll be there for a couple of weeks."

"I have two weeks' leave after I've been here a month. What a pity Paris is so far away," she said wistfully.

"Have you read the letter I sent on from your Kiwi?"

"Not yet. It came today. Maybe I should carry his picture around. I have some from Bath."

"That's a good idea as you are unlikely to see him again this side of ever."

Penny was smiling when she ended the call. The tension of the evening vanished and she showered and sat on the bed to read her letters. Jake wrote firmly, his thoughts put over well and, to her dismay, he was still vowing eternal love. "I've had time to think since coming home. My father was interested in the farming methods I saw on that video in Bath and wants someone to visit a ranch with him. He's semi-retired but keeps a finger in the pie and I said I'd go with him. It's fate, Penny. I knew I'd see you again and soon. We come over next week, first to Montana and then New York State, so take a break and come and meet me."

Thirteen

"Welcome to America." Penny had asked the driver to bring Liz to the hotel before she checked into the trailer park.

"It's wonderful! They really do have yellow cabs, just like on the films."

"You must be tired. I thought we'd have a light meal and a chat and then I'll take you over to the park."

"You shouldn't have gone to all this trouble, Penny. I know how busy you are. Josie is over the moon now that we have so much work in hand and she said to tell you she's thrilled with the two latest formal designs and the group of 'check and change' casuals for the mass market."

"This is a good place for work, Liz, but it's a relief to hear a really British voice again."

"When do I start?"

"Pat who lives in the trailer park close to your wagon will bring you over at lunch-time tomorrow. You'll need a long sleep to get over your jet lag and then you can work as hard as you feel inclined."

"I can't wait to see the workrooms. Do you see much of the stars?"

"Enough," Penny replied laconically. "Don't believe all you read in the press."

"I don't. I can't think that you'd fancy Lance Reaval. Not

after Chris. He came along to the workroom a couple of times with Josie and I thought he was wonderful."

"Why compare them? Chris and I have never had anything going and I'm not involved with anyone just now, even though Hector is very good-looking. Most girls pass out when they see him."

Liz laughed, her deep blue eyes glinting and lighting up her homely face. "Not you, and certainly not me. I watch the programme avidly but in real life I'd avoid such men. Your designs came over well on film – a lot of people have been impressed and given us orders."

"Clarrie is having fittings tomorrow afternoon so you'll meet her and maybe some of the production team." Almost certainly Karen Bruce.

Liz yawned and only picked at her food, so Penny took her to the trailer park and installed her in a very well-appointed wagon. She noticed that there was milk and bread and butter and a bowl of fruit to ease her into self-catering and a supply of packaged meals in the freezer.

"Whoever eats that?" Liz asked, eyeing a packet of frozen meatballs with distrust. "Is there a good grocery store or supermarket handy?"

"There's a big one just a block away and a good deli but Pat brought these things over to save you bothering with cooking."

"That was thoughtful, but I love cooking."

"You can give her anything you don't want. The studio paid for these and I know she can use them so you must do as you like."

"It's so exciting – I love all this. It's far nicer than my place in Islington. Did Josie tell you? Your friend Chris has taken it over while I'm in the States, so it was convenient for both of us."

"I thought he would be away in Europe."

"We all need somewhere to come back to, don't we? He'll use it between his travels and feel he's coming home."

Penny felt sad when she got back to her hotel. She had no place of her own. Looking back, she had never had a real home since her parents left England. Even that was the family home built to her parents' taste and holding their memories. She had never had a home of her own choosing. With Vincent and the others it had been an adventure in house-buying and a sexual experiment that was much less than satisfactory; and when the last piece of furniture and the last roll of carpet had gone, there had been no residual poignancy and sense of loss in the empty rooms. No lingering love for Vincent either; just a release into a kind of emotional limbo into which Jake and Chris had erupted, one with an onslaught of heady physical ego, and Chris with his more subtle and tender approach.

If I stay here, I'll rent an apartment. I'll live alone and invite only people I really like and trust.

Suddenly she was homesick for Josie and the girls in the workroom and the salon, the drab streets of Islington and the variety of the theatres in London. Her new room smelled of air freshener and spray polish and the windows were sealed for air-conditioning. The pictures were of rural scenes but otherwise the decor was exactly the same as in her first room.

She read the details of Jake's letter again. They would meet again soon and she felt no lifting of her spirits. The day he was expected in New York City was the day when she had to attend a big seminar where she was to speak about trends in fashion.

"You'll have to accept," Josie had insisted, even though it was going to be more like a historical lecture than a sales pitch, until the end when the latest models would be paraded. "It's an honour and it will bring a happy glow to the face of our bank manager. The fee is terrific and the potential sales after they see our gowns will be a fantastic boost to our economy. The trouble is that I want to be there and I'm far too busy. It's like being on a treadmill over here," she added with glee.

If he wants to see me he'll have to come to the seminar, Penny decided and chuckled. He'd stand out like a sore thumb, a fresh-faced athlete exuding sex, among the pallid men in suits and the precious drips who hung on the fringes of fashion and films. He might be so different that the film unit would "discover" him, a new virile man to make a few leading men anxious.

She looked at the folder she had compiled of pictures of fashion in the past and the sketches of what she predicted would be made in the near future, pictures that could be projected on a screen. Chris would do this better, she thought, and longed for some of the stills he'd shown her.

Liz was eager to start work and looked businesslike in jeans and blouson of dark blue with light red slip-on shoes. She looked round the enormous workroom and up at the wide high windows and sighed. "We could do with some of this space back home. Josie would go mad if she saw it."

"It's right for work but I miss a lot of British things."

"Everyone does. My cousin works in India and sends home pathetic letters asking for Mars Bars and Marmite."

Penny laughed. "I've met people like that, too. A friend from New Zealand is coming over with his father to look at cattle and may pay me a visit. The last time I saw him he was moaning that he couldn't get scones like his mother makes. Can you imagine anyone bothering with scones as a precious essential?"

"Yes, I can."

Penny looked up from the sketch on her pad and saw

that Liz was looking pensive. "I suppose you make the best scones this side of the Atlantic," she said with teasing irony.

"Maybe. I'm a very good cook. You must let me cook a meal for you if you can tear yourself away from lobster and nouvelle cuisine."

Penny pushed away the sketch pad and held a swatch of silk up to the light. "That could be useful, and you could do me a big favour."

"Like what? Do you need a special meal for someone?"

"Forget it. You haven't been here for five minutes and you need all your off-duty to see some of the sights of New York."

"There's time for that if I have a whole day off. I'll take one of the coach tours and do it all in one go."

"There's a lot to see."

"Not alone in a strange city. I'd rather cook for you so long as it isn't a cosy dinner for you and Lance Reaval. I'd poison him after all the lies he had printed in that magazine." She turned up her nose. "I bet he had a double for those stunts in the last series. It would be a pity to get his nice hair in a tizz."

"Jake, the friend I mentioned, said that the stunts were easy, so perhaps Hector managed to do them."

"Jake sounds good. Do I cook for him?"

"I have this seminar the day they arrive. I can't cancel it and they'll be left for a day before I can meet them. Karen said they can pick up a couple of visitor's cards from security and sit in on a filming session in the morning and some of the afternoon, after lunch with one of the producers, then there's a gap before they go back to their hotel for dinner." Penny bit the end of a pencil. "I could book them into a night-club or a musical, I suppose, but I have no idea what they'd like to see."

"You don't really know him."

"I do, but although I find him very attractive when I'm with him we don't agree on a lot of things and his lifestyle would drive me mad. He's an outdoor fanatic and he can't see the point of my job. I've never met his father, who farms sheep in a very big way, so I'll be out of my depth with him."

"I could give them tea in my trailer until they go back to their hotel, but I do plan a quick run round the park after tea each day. It gets dark late now so there's plenty of time."

"Are you sure? It's your time off."

"My pleasure."

"Take the next day off too. I employ you, not the studio, so I can give you extra days off if I choose to do so. If we work late for a day or so, we can both be clear for our separate appointments."

"Do you think I can watch the filming too? I want to see our dresses on the stars and my niece Yvonne wants some autographs."

"Sure. It's the least I can do, and thank you, Liz. You've taken a load off my mind."

It had done more than that. Penny inwardly confessed to a dread of meeting Jake again and this might make him realise that she was still a very busy lady with ideas of her own.

Pat cut out a shirt from a roll of soft grey panne velvet and tacked the edges loosely before it went to the machinist who sewed the first seams. Liz fingered an offcut and smiled. "May I have the bits? I brought a small portable machine with me and I hate having no needlework to do."

"Take what you want," Penny said carelessly, "but now I want you to look at the evening gown we've cut for Clarrie, as she's due for a fitting today."

Liz examined the garment tacked ready for the fitting.

"This is tricky stuff to handle, cut on the bias," she decided. "I'll do this one myself if that's all right with you, Pat?"

"What a relief." Pat stood watching the firm confident hands and sighed. "No wonder Penny had you come over. I was dreading sewing that one."

"This is a challenge but it'll be super and do a lot for our reputation," Liz said with satisfaction.

"Don't you do anything but work?" Pat asked in a disappointed voice as Liz carefully folded the offcuts of the materials used that day.

"I make small things for charity sales and my nieces like to have new dolls' clothes, but I take time to go walking and I've borrowed roller blades to try in the park."

"That sounds better. I like that but I hardly ever use them on my own."

"Come to tea today and then we can both go out in the park. Penny has friends coming over one day soon and I'm giving them tea, so on that day you can pop in for your afternoon break then we'll meet up after work and try the park again. They might want to join us."

"It all sounds far too energetic." Karen Bruce had been listening and Penny wondered what she thought of the new girl, but she discussed only the gowns and the fresh ideas that Penny had suggested and ignored the two assistants.

"She knows when she's not making headway," Pat whispered when Karen left. "Once she knows she has no chance with a girl she gives up and is as nice as pie."

"Do I invite her to tea?" Liz seemed to find her amusing. "I don't think she'd get on with your macho man, Penny."

"What macho man? You haven't invited Lance to tea?" Pat was horrified. "In that case I take a rain-check on tea."

"Jake is Penny's devoted boyfriend," or so Josie said. "He sounds terrific."

"Then put an extra cup for me," Pat replied with more enthusiasm.

Clarrie was delighted with the gown even in its early stages. "D'you know, I feel different in this; I even have to walk differently and I feel a million dollars."

"You look wonderful," Liz said. "I can't wait to see the other clothes." Her deft fingers adjusted a seam and she pinned a pleat to neaten the waistband. "There! That's it for today."

"They need it as soon as possible, or so Karen said."

"It'll be ready before I have my day off," Liz reassured her.

"I want to go over my notes for the seminar," Penny frowned. "There's so much to do. I'll grab a coffee and a sandwich and look in here again later."

"We can tidy up and see to security," Pat offered. "We've nearly finished the urgent items."

"Bless you both. Have fun falling over in the park."

She glanced back at the absorbed expressions of the two girls bent over their work. Pat was really pretty, and even Liz looked good with her friendly smile and bright eyes. Pat was lively and, from what she'd told Penny about holidays she'd taken with her ex-boyfriend, adventurous. Maybe she would fall for Jake. He could do a lot worse.

She felt safe, as she knew that Hector was working in the studio and the reporter seemed to have decided that she was more trouble than she was worth. He had not been seen for two days and a health scandal in the food industry had taken the front pages.

"Message for you, Miss Wallace." The girl in reception spoke nervously, as if Penny would eat her up and spit out the bones.

Penny took the memo slip and nodded. "If he rings again

I shall be in my room for at least two hours." She braced herself for an awkward few minutes when Jake contacted her. She could imagine his face and the hurt and resentful expression when she told him that she had other plans for the day of his arrival, but to her surprise he accepted the fact that she was busy.

"Dad will be thrilled to see them making the soap. He and mother are big fans and if he can get some autographs he will flip."

"I have it all fixed for you to pick up security cards at the gate and Pat and Liz, two of my girls, will look after you both when the session is over. By the way, do you go roller blading?"

"I don't believe it. Penny on a roller?"

"Don't sound so surprised. I can do it but I haven't the time. Pat and Liz can take you if you want to join them. Pat is a bit of an outdoor girl and is looking forward to meeting you."

Oh dear, I sound as if I'm match-making, and I am!

"She sounds fine, but it's you I came to see." There was silence for a ponderous moment. "I thought we'd never get together again, Penny, but when Dad suggested this trip, I knew I had to settle a few matters once and for all. He knew it too, as I told him how I feel about you. I know he'll love you."

"It will be good to see you, but I haven't changed, and my work seems to be taking over my life. Have you started work with your sheep, Jake?"

"It's going like a dream, and my house is finished except for the furniture and drapes and things."

"That's wonderful."

"Yeah, wonderful but empty. It lacks a woman's touch. Hell, Penny, I need to be married! I have to see you soon."

"Where are you now?"

He sighed. "Too far away. We're still in Montana looking at cattle, but we've booked our hotel in New York, not far from you." He told her the name and she made a note of the phone number. "See you soon, Penny. Thanks for telling me about the park. I can use some exercise. I'll buy the equipment before I get to you."

Dear Jake, for him the important part of his itinerary would be scooting about in the park – apart from seeing her, of course.

Penny closed her folder after another hour of concentrated work, confident that her notes were complete, and she wondered what the time was in Paris. She rang reception and asked the girl to look at the huge array of clock faces in the lobby, each with the time of day in a major capital of the world. Penny thanked her and found her diary. Why not? Josie had urged her to write to Chris but she had torn up several weak attempts and couldn't face another. Maybe he would be out, maybe she could leave a bright message, maybe she would make a fool of herself. It was early in the morning in Paris. Maybe he was still in bed.

She giggled. He *is* in bed! She heard the sleepy voice say, "Yes?"

"Get up, you lazy so-and-so."

"Penny?" He was slightly more alert now, but she felt that she had the advantage, being fully awake and dressed. Shoes gave her confidence and she wondered fleetingly if he slept naked.

"It's dawn! Or some might call it morning. Do you sleep with the drapes drawn back from the windows, Penny?"

"Sometimes. Why?"

"If you were here we could have croissants and coffee in bed and watch the sunrise. I can see Notre Dame from this bed and the Hunter of the East has caught the Sultan's turret in a noose of light. It's all pink," he added in a matter-of-fact voice that dismissed Omar's imagery.

"Hallo," she said weakly. "How is Paris?"

"Fine now. Fine at any time but now I am happy."

"I just rang . . ."

"To say you love me?"

"No, of course not. Just a friendly greeting. It's a relief to speak to a friend after being bombarded by Yankee voices all day."

"Just Americans? Josie said that Jake was on his way to see you."

"Josie is a big-mouth!"

"Josie is my good friend and so is Liz. I don't need you as a friend."

"I need you as my friend."

"Why, Penny?" He sounded serious. "Are you so scared of Jake, of your own hormones and his force of personality that you need to hide?"

"A little."

"You won't take me so you'll have to make do with St Christopher. I hope he saved you from Lance Reaval."

"That was an easy one."

"Do I detect a certain ruthlessness? First Vincent and then the great sex king himself, in spite of what I read in the magazines."

"That wasn't true. Hector is fun but I have no time for him away from the set."

"Truly?"

"You believed that crap?"

"I believed what I saw: that you enjoyed his company," he said mildly.

She told him about the seminar and he suggested a few references on Elizabethan dresses that she could look up.

"I wish you were here. I need you," she murmured.

"What was that?"

"Nothing, Chris. I must go now. Think of me at the seminar."

"As always," he said politely and put down his phone.

Penny wished that she had not telephoned him. It was good to hear his voice but she was restless now and she should have said a lot more or a lot less. She did want him to be with her, as a friend, as a colleague and as a very wonderful guy.

Fourteen

"Penny?"

"Did you have a good day, Liz? Anything wrong? Didn't they turn up to watch the filming?"

It was after eleven at night and Penny was ready to fall into bed. The seminar had been a success and she knew that if she was asked to do more lectures, as several parties hinted, she must have an agent or another manager who would deal with all the matters that Josie avoided. When she heard Liz she had to drag her mind back to Jake and his father Steve Morgan.

"I know it's late but Jake said he wanted to meet you for breakfast at your hotel, so I promised I'd warn you to expect him and his father about nine." She sounded amused. "They were tired and I think they'd eaten too much. Jake tried to ring you but you were out, so they've gone to bed. They want to be up bright and early tomorrow."

"I hope you weren't bored. I've not met Steve and I thought he might be limited as far as social graces are concerned."

"No way! Pat and I had a great time in the park and they seemed to enjoy their tea." She giggled. "I'm glad you mentioned scones." Liz seemed to be on edge. "You did say I could have tomorrow off?"

"Yes, and I want you to have dinner with Jake and his father and me here in the evening. Have they said what they want to do for the rest of the day?" Guiltily, Penny recalled that she'd made no plans for them to cover the time when she had to work and she had a long appointment with the director of the wardrobe department. "They can't expect me to spend a lot of time with them. They know I'm working and I didn't invite them here."

"That's OK," Liz sounded relieved. "They asked me to go on a tour of New York with them and I said I would if you had no other plans."

"I'm grateful. I do have to be here for most of the day and breakfast is a good idea. We can all meet again for dinner. Did Pat get on with them?"

"She fell for both of them. She thinks that Jake is the best-looking man she's seen."

"And you? Did you like them?"

"They were so easy, like family. Good-night, Penny, and thank you."

"For what?" she asked. "It's you who helped me out of a tight situation." But Liz had hung up and didn't hear.

At six a.m. Penny was wide awake and had butterflies about meeting Jake. His father will be here too, so he can't get too intense, she thought with relief. The reporter from a prestigious newspaper wanted to have lunch with the four main stars, Karen Bruce and, as they said, the intriguing new designer, Penny Wallace, so she dressed with care and knew that she would be expected to be elegant in one of her own creations.

To be the first at the breakfast table in the main dining-room gave her an advantage. The huge room was beautifully appointed but the walk from the door to the table could be formidable, as walking down a long church aisle had been when she was a bridesmaid, knowing that everyone was watching her. She'd be hopeless on the catwalk.

Jake paused in the entrance and when he saw Penny

he smiled his delight and hurried forward, not abashed by luxury or distance, and she stood up to be seized in a crushing hug that was likely to crumple her suit. Steve followed slowly, and Penny sensed that she was being regarded with grave interest and the assessing gaze that he reserved for only the best thoroughbred cattle.

"You look wonderful," Jake said at last, after gazing at her with a kind of awe. "Isn't she just wonderful, Dad?"

"Don't know when I've met a prettier woman, and you surely do know how to dress up," his father admitted. Penny looked at him sharply and met his gaze. He shook his head slightly at some private thought and she knew that, even if he never voiced his feelings about her, he was disappointed.

Jake ordered pancakes, maple syrup, bacon and sausages and two fried eggs. Steve ordered the same but Penny had coffee and toast.

"No fries?" Steve asked, the first of any comments since his first greeting.

"Not this early in the day. I have a business lunch and I must save space for that."

"Penny likes to keep her figure," Jake remarked, almost in apology.

"I eat very well," she protested.

"Yeah, I know. Two whole Maids of Honour tarts." He seemed nostalgic. "Bath was a great city."

"You didn't think so when you were there."

"I did when I met you."

"It was the river and the scones that you liked, and the whitebait."

"That girl Liz makes good scones," Steve said. He contemplated his son as if he hoped his madness would subside, and Penny shared the feeling.

"Liz and Pat were delighted that you joined them in the park. It sounded like fun."

"They are terrific and to cap it all, Liz made us a really good feed with scones and cream and cheese flan so we stayed there watching rugby on the box and then had supper there as well."

"I thought you might take her out to dinner."

"She said she had a casserole on the go, so we stayed," Steve said. "Fluffy dumplings and a bit of taste to it."

"Well, tonight I can't offer you that, but the food is good here and Liz will join us at eight if that suits you."

Steve laughed. "Suits me. Can't see you behind a skillet, Penny." He pushed aside his plate and stood up. "I have a few phone calls to make before we pick up Liz. We said we'd take her on the town today to say thank you. I decided on those steers, Jake, so the sooner they are shipped home the better." He nodded to her and left, leaving the impression that he would like to ship Jake out with the steers.

"Dad's a bit brusque," Jake said. "Maybe you should have worn jeans."

"And have to change again as soon as Steve left?" Her eyebrows arched with irony. "I have a full morning and a business lunch with the press. This is my life, Jake. I wear what suits the occasion. In Bath it was holiday casual clothes but here I have to look smart at all times."

He eyed her hungrily but with a tinge of sadness. "I love you, Penny. I had to see you again to make sure I can make the right decision. Seeing you like this makes me know you were right. You are the angel on top of the Christmas tree, and I'm not tall enough to reach you. I know that you will never marry me and I know that I shall never love another woman as I love you, but I've had time to think."

"You'll forget me, Jake. You must forget me."

He looked away, agonised by her now gentle face. "Never, and I hope you remember me sometimes."

"Is this goodbye? What about our dinner date?"

"Not goodbye and we are both looking forward to this evening." He smiled. "Dad is a devious old devil but he makes sense. I need a wife who will fit into our lives and become one of the family." He laughed wryly. "I nearly hit him when he first said that, but now, seeing you again, looking like something out of *Vogue*, I know it can never be for me. In a way I'm glad I am in love with you. I know that I can stop looking for perfection. I found that in you. It will never happen again, so I can marry a nice girl and be happy and keep my mind on what really matters to the farm, the family and my own future." She noticed a new hardness in his mouth and mourned for the boy with the light heart.

When he smiled, the hardness disappeared. "They say that lightning never strikes the same place twice, so I've had my burning bolt and it means that there's no danger of me going off the rails after I'm married. It can never happen again. I shall see things clearly and my marriage will survive."

"Are you going to marry the girl your family wanted for you?" She looked shocked. "You don't even like her. Don't waste yourself on just anyone, Jake. You are worth more than that."

"Not her! Leave it out!"

"But there is someone?"

"Maybe. Isn't it time that you went to work? See you this evening."

Briefly, she touched his hand. "Have fun with the girls."

"Pat's working today. It's just Liz."

"Hard luck."

"Yeah. Pat reminds me of my cousin, as pretty as paint and good at sport. She's got a nice smile too."

Penny had seen Pat's interest in meeting the attractive Kiwi and knew that she was raw from her break-up with Mike, after a year of frantic sex that had suddenly cooled for both of them, as if the fire had died without even a smouldering of ashes. She hoped that Jake wouldn't think of Pat as a suitable wife. Penny made a wry face. A suitable wife? Who could fill that position for a good-looking, virile and very chauvinistic man who would expect a woman to give him love and service and allow him to rule her life? If Jake did anything in a hurry, and she knew how impulsive he could be, he wouldn't have time to discover that Pat was completely bemused by saucepans and recipes.

No reporters or cameramen lurked in the lobby, and when Penny left the hotel she was full of plans for the day. A fax from Josie covered a few queries about fabrics and Pat was busy teaching a new girl the workings of the department while sewing machines droned peacefully and under Penny's skilled fingers a new design burst into being.

The inner tension faded and Penny knew that she was doing what she wanted to do and had no need for Jake, Vincent or anyone in America. Coffee came in a large vacuum flask and Penny watched the girls at work while she sipped a scalding cup of the brew that was rapidly becoming addictive. But as her concentration on the design slipped, she felt empty. It wasn't true. She did need someone to whom she could turn and smile and hold close and share. Stupid bitch, she thought angrily. You don't know what you really want.

Before lunch, she went on the set and made a few notes. Hector smiled cautiously, still unable to believe that she had given him the elbow even before he had persuaded her that sex with him would be a revelation.

Vincent came over and sat by her chair but said little, as if he knew that any approach would be hopeless. "I heard that your boyfriend had arrived," he said, as if accusing her of a crime that he hoped she would deny.

"Jake? Yes he's here." She looked at him sideways. "He's very sweet and *so* attractive. We had a long and serious talk at breakfast this morning." Her smile hinted that Jake had been with her all night and she had enjoyed it. "We had a lot to discuss."

"I've been signed up for the next series," Vincent said. "Are you staying on or going to live in New Zealand?"

For a moment she stared at him, unable to see the implication, then said hastily, "No plans as yet but a lot of my work has been done, unless they change the cast drastically. The girls here have been wonderful. Soon I may be able to send Liz back to Josie, who's yelling for her, and I may be free to go back to London for a while."

"Work! Always your work," Vincent said bitterly. "Success has gone to your head, Penny. Have you ever wondered if it will last?"

"Who knows? Do you have confidence in your own future, Vincent?" She sensed his unwilling awareness of her and his resentment that he had no part in her success so she hardened her heart. "Why not marry a rich widow who doesn't need a torrid love affair, and settle down."

He stood up, shaking with anger. "I don't need you, Penny. I can make my own way, even if you get all the publicity. I doubt if many men would want you when they know what you are really like. Hector said you must be frigid and I agreed. I should know!"

"Goodbye, Vincent. I need this space." She turned away and opened a magazine that had two of her gowns on the centre page. Success was good but it had its bitter side. Steve eyed her as if she was a pretty, over-dressed doll with no real sense, and Jake admitted that she wouldn't fit into his life. Hector looked as if he was on the hunt again, panting after the newest member of the cast, a curvaceous redhead with bold eyes who would make the anorexic actors look merely thin and sexless and who would be sensational in the dresses designed for her.

Elizabeth Daish

I don't want any of them, so why do I feel empty? I have followed Gertrude's advice and avoided taking a lover just to fill a gap, so I have only myself to blame if I am alone.

Karen Bruce smiled when she saw Penny making a pretence at eating the chicken tarragon and pushed her own plate away. "Don't you wish they'd go easy on the food?"

"I have a dinner date, so I really can't eat this sort of food twice in one day."

"I saw your date yesterday when he came to the set. If looks could kill, both Hector and Vincent would be for the electric chair."

Penny laughed. "They loved seeing the cast in session and Liz told me that someone suggested that they introduce a new sub-hero fresh from the sheep farm, oozing bucolic sex and causing havoc among the females."

"Do you think Jake would be interested?"

"Definitely not. He has his own life and loves it."

"He'd be with you."

"No, he will go back to New Zealand with his father and get on with farming."

"Well, you couldn't send sheep through a dip in that rig." Karen laughed. "I can't imagine you in a hands-on farm role, dear."

"You are so right. His father will be glad to see the back of me and I have no plans to emigrate."

"What will you do when you finish here?"

"I've agreed to come over twice a year as a consultant for a month at a time to make sure they are keeping to my schedule and not cutting corners. I can assess what the cast needs, rough out the designs and finish them in London."

"I may come over to visit you." Karen grinned. "Not like that. I have found a nice little girl who fits in to my life and I'm really fond of her, so everyone can relax. Karen Bruce

172

is not hunting for little dykes any more. She's sweet and she can cook."

"Come over, and bring her too." They regarded each other with real warmth. "I'm glad we've worked together, Karen."

"Me too. I have so few women friends. Real friend-friends with no hang-ups."

They discussed future work, Penny refusing to take on more than she and Josie could realistically manage, but planned a launch of casual sports wear for the mass market, even agreeing to a "His and Hers" range that would be popular in the States.

At five o'clock, Penny sank on to the bed in her room, mentally exhausted. She set her alarm for seven and dozed, then showered and looked for something to wear. She wanted to slip into something light and casual, with low heels and a loose waistline, but instinct told her to be more formal as Jake might have second thoughts if she appeared as he'd seen her in England, more accessible and sweet.

The silvery sheath dress and gold and pearl chain necklace was a compromise of deceptive simplicity, and the silver sandals made the picture complete. Perfume and skilful make-up added to the "look but don't touch" aura, and she smiled, satisfied that Jake would not dare to kiss her apart from a peck on the cheek.

The two men had the appearance of scrubbed care. Penny couldn't smell carbolic soap but she was sure that Steve used it a lot. Jake smelled of lavishly applied aftershave and his eyes were bright with humour. Liz wore a floral blue shirt and pleated skirt and looked almost pretty. Her hair was soft and shining and there was natural colour in her cheeks.

"I'm starving," Jake said.

It was a greeting that Penny could understand. She relaxed, and they ordered the food while drinking cocktails that, surprisingly, Steve wanted to try. Penny watched Steve talking to Liz and saw that they slotted in together as if they'd known each other for years.

"If you farm sheep, why buy steers?" Liz wanted to know.

"I turn steers out on the fields before the sheep go in to graze," Steve explained.

"Don't they eat all the grass?"

"Cattle eat only the tops of the grass, never down far on the stalks and never to ground level. They eat all the pests that cling to the tops of long grass. It doesn't hurt them but they eat all the bugs that could infect sheep. It means that when they go in, there is clean grazing and I never have to use chemicals after the first few months as lambs. So they are free of the fluke and other diseases and when they go to market there is no residual chemical in the meat. We use the steers for meat or sell young ones we've fattened up. A good steak on the barbie goes down a treat."

Jake watched Penny watching Liz and Steve. "They get on well. We all do," he said quietly and grinned. "Thought I'd make sure and test out Liz, so I took her to a fun fair while Dad shopped for my mother's present. We went through the Tunnel of Love twice."

Penny giggled. "You realise I should hate you. Liz is the best dressmaker I have."

"Tough luck! You owe me, Penny."

"What happens now?"

Jake raised his voice so that the others could hear. "Dad and me want to see Canada while we're here. We'll take the train across and drive back."

"That takes a long time."

"About three weeks we reckon," Steve said. "That will give Liz time to pack and get a visa and come with us for a holiday."

Penny nodded. "Liz hasn't had a holiday for at least eighteen months."

"It's OK?" Liz sounded uncertain.

"Take your time. Take for ever but make sure you do what you really want to do. If you need to come back, there will be a job for you."

Liz smiled but her eyes were over-bright. "I may have time to make you a quilt. Jake told me about Bath. I'd make it on a machine, not by hand, using all those gorgeous offcuts I gathered. I might sell some, too."

Steve smiled at Penny, a real smile that made him look like Jake. "You're a good girl, Penny." He yawned. "Bed for me, so come on boy, say good-night to Penny and I'll get a cab to take Liz back to the trailer first before we go on to our hotel. These young ladies have to work tomorrow and we have to book our tour if we are to get it all in."

Penny walked with Jake and Liz to reception to see if she had any messages. He held her lightly and kissed her cheeks. "Goodbye, Angel."

"Goodbye, Jake. Take good care of her. She's a gem."

"I know."

Steve called from the foyer and Jake seized Liz by the hand and rushed her away to the cab.

Penny took the letters and a fax to her room as her eyes were too misty to read them in the foyer. Once there, she flung the papers on the desk and decided that she had done enough for one day. She peeled off the silvery gown, brushed her teeth and removed her make-up, then slipped naked into bed and was asleep in two minutes.

Fifteen

The wake-up call that was now a daily routine purred discreetly as if apologising for existing, and Penny woke from a heavy sleep feeling as if she was emerging from a deep pit. The St Christopher chain dug into her neck. It was all that she had worn in bed. The shower sent needle sprays of hot water over her body, shocking enough to wake the moribund and she washed her face in cold water.

A work day, and peace from official lunches or interviews, she recollected with relief, and she took her time over breakfast, the papers from last night by her side plate. There was a redirected letter from her relatives in Canada. It reminded her that she might like to tell Liz to pass on their address in case Jake and Steve were anywhere near on their trip. The letter was full of family news with no hint of a visit back to England so there was no urgency for a reply.

The fax made her sit up straight. Josie still seemed to think that messages sent in this way were almost in code. "Warning," she said. "Chris back from France and on the move again soon." A few more-practical messages followed, with a plea for Penny to come back and sort out some problems in the workrooms.

I could go back before it hots up again when filming begins for the next series, she thought. I've done my part for this series, the girls are very efficient and Pat understands my designs. She wondered if Chris was visiting Gertrude and Lars and envied him. She fingered the St Christopher medallion and tried to imagine his face. He might have waited for me! We were both invited. She felt resentful. She had heard nothing from him since phoning him in Paris. Josie had seen him, and so had Liz before he went to Paris, but not even a picture postcard for her.

It was the fault of those pictures in the magazines. He had really believed all he read in the papers about her and Hector. She arrived in the workroom feeling sad and restless.

Liz greeted her with a wide smile, a gentle radiance lighting her eyes. "We are going to get married in New Zealand," she said. "I know he is in love with you, Penny, but he loves me too and in time he will be a fine husband and father." She saw Penny's doubts. "It's what I want and you've set him free. You showed him that you were . . . unattainable. You don't know how generous that makes you."

"Not generous at all, Liz. Can you imagine me out there watching cattle take the tops off grass and making scones?" Her laugh was hollow. "Come on, if you are deserting me we have work to do."

"You had your message?"

"Yes, I had a fax from Josie."

"So you know that Chris is back?"

"How did *you* know?"

"He has my flat and he telephoned."

"I see."

Penny picked up a pen and doodled on a pad. The result was not promising and she tore it up. "I need some coffee."

"You need fresh air. You haven't been outside air-conditioned rooms for days."

"You're right. What happened to my green spaces?"

"What?"

"It's just something I thought I needed but I never get. You'll have your green spaces – miles of it – but for me it wouldn't be my space and might even be claustrophobic," Penny said regretfully.

"You need your own space, but enclosed by things you love like old buildings and history."

"Why are you so wise, Liz?"

"You also need a real love to make it all green and fresh."

"Now you are getting fanciful. What it is to be in love! Where is that girl with my coffee?"

Penny had an inward vision of Liz as an immigrant girl going to New Zealand in the last century, when a man came to the boats and picked out a wife who could do all the necessary chores and be a comfort and helper in every way, the union untroubled by romantic love.

Love would come later and be as deep in shared experience of work, joy and sadness as any that had been found in a match born of social meeting and physical attraction. Liz knew what was expected of her and welcomed the challenge, so long as her husband would be kind and healthy and give her status and nice babies and enough home comforts to keep her contented. It would be a partnership.

Penny looked at the last lines she'd sketched. Work was spasmodic and when it was time to pack away her pens and paper she wondered if she had wasted the whole day.

She had a sudden desire for British fish and chips with vinegar and salt and a glass of Guinness, but knew that the American substitute would be a poor imitation, so she settled for the healthier alternative of salmon and salad in the small dining-room at the hotel.

Karen had agreed that a break might be good for her and a meeting was arranged to tie up loose ends with the wardrobe and production. "Get away for a week or two and come back with even more ideas. We can't lose you now, you're a hot property," the director assured her, and the thought of a short holiday among familiar places was exciting enough to make her have renewed energy at work.

A week went by and Liz heard from Jake, passing on warm greetings and saying that they were having a ball. "I shall be away when they come to fetch you, Liz," Penny said casually. "Remember to write and send me pictures of the wedding."

"I'll do that and I'll never forget what you've done for me." Liz smiled wickedly. "It was the scones that did it. Pat was livid, as she can't even boil an egg. So she had no chance whatsoever unless it was for a one-night stand!"

"What a thing to say about your beloved!"

"He's a man and a Kiwi and I'm not daft. I've made it clear that there will be none of that in the future or I shall come back here."

"You actually said that?"

"Not in so many words, but he got the message that it will be all or nothing between us. There are ways of making men think they have the ultimate power but the poor saps can be pointed in the right direction. I should know. My father could be a bit heavy-handed if he felt like it, but Mother was wise and good humoured and somehow he ended up agreeing with her and boasting that it was all his idea."

"So it runs in the family?"

"Jake is getting a bargain," Liz said calmly. "He is marrying a virgin who can cook and sew and will enjoy making love and having babies."

"So you haven't?"

"Of course not," Liz replied primly, then laughed. "He was quite overcome when I refused a try-out and he's intrigued that virgins still exist. I'm not pretty so I have to make the most of my assets and see that he values them."

"Poor Jake. He doesn't know what's hit him, but you will make him happy."

"That's my side of the bargain," Liz said simply. "I shall be the perfect wife for him, but please don't visit us until after I have my first baby. By that time it will be safe for him to see you again," she added shrewdly.

"I shan't be here when you leave."

"Thanks, Penny. Now get on with your own life and find your space. Vincent was a mistake and has left you on the defensive." She turned away and murmured, "Pride is a sour companion." She folded a length of cloth and put it on a pile with the others. "When does your flight arrive at Heathrow?"

"It isn't important."

"I think it is. I remember the sheer relief I felt when the cab driver was standing there holding a card with my name on it on my arrival here. I'll ask the unit's travel people to set it up for you over there."

Penny gave her details of the flight number and times of departure and arrival and concentrated all her attention on packing the mass of luggage that had grown alarmingly during her stay in New York. Some she stored and locked in a spare cupboard in the workroom and felt a sense of belonging. With satisfaction she thought, I shall come back. I have small roots growing here and it will all be familiar when I return.

Josie was delighted. "About time too," she asserted over the phone, as if she was cross that Penny had been away for so long. "You needn't think you are coming back for a rest. I have a list of 'must dos' as long as my arm. How do you feel about designing kids' clobber?"

"I don't know any children and I need a rest."

"You can have a week on your own," Josie offered grudgingly, "but as far as I can see, you will have to camp out again in the studio or go to a hotel."

"I'm getting used to hotel service, so book me into the nearest one with room service and nice towels."

"I said you'd never settle for the outback."

"The outback is Australia. To whom were you sounding off about me?" she asked with dignity. "As you know, I've missed my chances and he's marrying Liz."

"Good! Great for a roll in the hay but not for keeps."

"You are the pits! I haven't time for men just now. Everyone, including you, conspires to keep me so busy I hardly raise my head above the desk."

"You should feast your eyes on the last bank statement, ducky. I want to talk about investments."

"Give yourself a raise," Penny said dryly.

"That too, and I'm worth it."

"You certainly are, but I can go off people who get big-headed."

When she turned away from the phone, Penny was smiling. It would be relaxing to exchange mild off-beat insults with Josie and the girls in the salon again in a way she found impossible in the States. She was taken very seriously and viewed with a kind of awed reserve by most of the work staff.

She packed presents for a few friends and gave Liz a generous cheque for a leaving present. Liz tucked it into her purse and smiled. "It's too much but I shall take it with pleasure. I shall keep the money with my own savings. Every girl needs something of her own for a rainy day."

"Will it ever rain on you?"

"I hope not, but I have to keep something of my own. Complete dependence isn't good."

Her car waited as she followed the bellboy with the luggage. She looked back at the hotel that had taken her into its luxurious impersonal embrace and now pushed her out with never a regret. She wondered if the next occupant of the room would like the paintings under the hooded lights and wished she'd had the courage to turn them face to the wall while she was there.

On the plane she put on dark glasses and took out a paperback, defences against the self-assurance of a minor pop star who sat next to her in Club Class. She wrinkled her nose. He unpacked his freebie pack with the delight of a child under the Christmas tree and took off his trainers, letting a smell of socks and sweat emanate before he pulled on the grey comfort socks supplied in the pack.

Penny turned her face away and tried to sleep, the do-not-disturb sign on her blanket discouraging conversation and offers of food and drink, and the hours slipped by.

Far above the earth, she was suspended between two parts of her life, between similar but separate cultures and ideas, and between hotels that would seem the same, as airports were the same wherever she went in the sohphisticated cities she must visit.

She slept and woke to find the man next to her was drinking more champagne and eating the second meal of the night but she shook her head when the steward offered her refreshment. Almost light-headed from the flight and possibly from lack of food she waited for her cases by the carousel and then pushed her trolley out to find her driver.

The smell of traffic exhaust and the patina of soft rain was almost welcome as the car took her to the hotel that Josie had selected, where a smallish mahogany and velvet lounge and a pleasant room with a wide window overlooking a triangle of park awaited her.

She sank into a warm bath and then opened a case. No need to dress up until tomorrow when she would go to the salon and meet Josie for lunch. She found her soft blue moccasins and a trouser suit of grey and pale blue and shook out the creases in her showerproof coat.

She was hungry and felt no jet lag, as she had slept quite well on the plane. She knew the area and tried to decide if the Italian place would be better than the Chinese restaurant round the corner, dismissing the hotel as mundane so far as food was concerned.

The house phone was much more shrill than the smooth tones in New York and she picked up the receiver with a sense of shock.

"A caller for you, Miss Wallace."

"Put her through." She smiled. Nice of Josie to say hallo.

"A caller *here* in the bar, Miss Wallace, not on the phone."

Better still. Josie was always hungry and they could eat together. She snatched up her coat and purse and ran down the stairs.

Chris sat on a bar stool and twisted round when she came into the room. "I thought you were away," she said weakly.

"I don't think I am," he replied seriously, and slid off the stool to kiss her cheeks, continental style.

"How did you know I was here?"

"Liz and Josie seem to like me and keep me informed. Liz told me when the plane would come in but I thought you'd like to unpack before I take you out this evening. If you have eaten everything in sight on the plane, you can watch me eat – I'm starving."

"So am I. I slept and tried not to smell the feet of the man next to me."

"That's what I like. Straight into an intellectual conversation after we've been parted for so long."

Tension eased and Penny began to giggle. "Oh Chris, I've missed you."

"I nearly came over after you called Paris."

"But you saw the pictures?"

"The competition seemed overwhelming but I heard or thought I heard a whisper just before you rang off."

"What?"

"Wish you were here . . . so I waited until the dust settled and came back so that I could come over when I thought you might want me."

"But you didn't," she said flatly.

"I had an SOS from Liz telling me to stay put as you were coming back. Anyone want an air ticket, unused?"

"You can trade it in for another."

"Maybe two to Sweden? It's summer now and they will be delighted to see us, or so I hear."

"I have a week off."

"I know."

"You are maddening. You seem to know everything, but you *can* get the tickets. I want to see Gertrude again."

"I already have them. We leave tomorrow."

"You were sure I'd come?"

"No, but I hoped so. Come and eat before I die of hunger and love."

"I love you too," she said quietly. "Chinese or Italian?"